Night of the Toads

■ ■ ■

*#3 in the Edgar Award-winning
Dan Fortune mystery series*

Dennis Lynds

Originally published under the pseudonym Michael Collins

Night of the Toads e-book edition: 978-1-941517-04-8
Night of the Toads POD edition: 978-1-941517-05-5

For inquiries:
Gayle Lynds
P.O. Box 732
125 Forest Avenue
Portland, ME 04101-9998
www.DennisLynds.com

To Marty Booher,
a big man and a good friend

Acclaim for Dennis Lynds & His Novels

"Tough, believable." – *San Francisco Examiner*

"[Lynds] handles an excellent and complex plot with ease." – *The Washington Star*

"Really moving ... emotional soundness without sentimentality." – *San Francisco Chronicle*

"In the American private-eye tradition of Chandler, Hammett, and Macdonald." – *The New York Times Book Review*

"The man who won the Mystery Writers of America award ... has given readers another exceptional story." – *Parade of Books*

"Skillfully plotted with finely honed suspense." – *New York Times*

"[Lynds] is a writer to watch and above all to read." – Ross Macdonald

"A master of crime fiction." – *Ellery Queen Mystery Magazine*

"Smashing ... leaves the reader breathless." – *Publishers Weekly*

"[Lynds's books are] filled with as much closely observed incident and detail as John O'Hara short stories." – *Wall Street Journal*

"First-class ... suspenseful, character-rich, and absorbing." – *Kirkus Reviews*

"Some of the rawest, most unencumbered mystery writing extant in the genre." – *American Library Association*

"[He] carries on the Hammett-Chandler-Macdonald tradition with skill and finesse." – *Washington Post Book World*

"... combines superb characters and excellent plotting." – *ALA Booklist*

"... powerful writing." – *Library Journal*

"... engrossing and empathic." – *New York Daily News*

"... hot mystery writer whose novels have reached mainstream status. ..." – *San Diego Reporter*

"Collins is the Costa-Gavras of the PI world ... we might also call him the Captain Kirk of PI writers, boldly taking the genre where no colleague has gone before – and doing it so passionately that we can't help but sign on for the quest with him." – literary critic Francis M. Nevins, Jr.

"Lynds is a major contributor to the form, even a redefiner of it; whether or not he is ever given his just due, he should take satisfaction from the fact that he has written mystery novels of genuine distinction." – literary critic Richard Carpenter

Dan Fortune series, by Dennis Lynds, originally published under the pseudonym Michael Collins

Act of Fear, 1967
The Brass Rainbow, 1969
Night of the Toads, 1970
Walk a Black Wind, 1971
Shadow of a Tiger, 1972
The Silent Scream, 1973
Blue Death, 1975
The Blood-Red Dream, 1976
The Nightrunners, 1978
The Slasher, 1980
Freak, 1983
Minnesota Strip, 1987
Red Rosa, 1988
A Dangerous Job, 1989
Chasing Eights, 1990
The Irishman's Horse, 1991
Cassandra In Red, 1992

Paul Shaw series, by Dennis Lynds, originally published under the pseudonym Mark Sadler

The Falling Man, 1970
Here to Die, 1971
Mirror Image, 1972
Circle of Fire, 1973
Touch of Death, 1981
Deadly Innocents, 1986

Kane Jackson series, by Dennis Lynds, originally published under the pseudonym William Arden

A Dark Power, 1968
Deal in Violence, 1969
The Goliath Scheme, 1971

Die to a Distant Drum, 1972
Deadly Legacy, 1973

Buena Costa County series, by Dennis Lynds, originally published under the pseudonym John Crowe
Another Way to Die, 1972
A Touch of Darkness, 1972
Bloodwater, 1974
Crooked Shadows, 1975
When They Kill Your Wife, 1977
Close to Death, 1979

George Malcolm, private detective, by Dennis Lynds, originally published under the pseudonym Carl Dekker
Woman in Marble, 1973

Langford ("Ford") Morgan, ex-soldier, ex-CIA, ex-roustabout, by Dennis Lynds, originally published under the pseudonym Michael Collins
The Cadillac Cowboy, 1995

Other of his works include science fiction novels, literary novels, mystery short stories, literary short stories, short story anthologies, and poetry.

Table of Contents

Chapter 1 1
Chapter 2 7
Chapter 3 14
Chapter 4 20
Chapter 5 26
Chapter 6 34
Chapter 7 41
Chapter 8 47
Chapter 9 52
Chapter 10 60
Chapter 11 67
Chapter 12 73
Chapter 13 79
Chapter 14 86
Chapter 15 93
Chapter 16 100
Chapter 17 107
Chapter 18 115
Chapter 19 121
Chapter 20 127
Chapter 21 132
Chapter 22 139
Chapter 23 147
Chapter 24 153

Chapter 25... 160
Chapter 26... 163
Sneak Peek at the next Dan Fortune Mystery............................. 173
Meet the Author: Dennis Lynds 177
The Back Cover.. 181

1

I'D NEVER have remembered the girl if Ricardo Vega had been another man. He wasn't. He was "Rey" Vega to anyone who claimed to
know him well—*El Rey*, the King.

We don't admit it, but we consider a successful man a better man.
A prince of success, an inevitable winner. Maybe it's only that we never lost our need for princes, and if we don't have an aristocracy, we
make one. An aristocracy is comforting. It takes us off the hook—we
never really had a chance to make it big. At the same time, of course,
since an aristocracy of success isn't really closed to us, we can all
dream. A contradiction, sure, but logic has never bothered people's
attitudes much.

The trouble is that the successful man himself has a way of coming to believe he is better. From there it's an almost automatic step
to believing he was always better—born better, a different breed of
man. A man who should have rights and privileges ordinary men don't
have. A special man, superior, a king. That was Ricardo Vega. I didn't
know him well enough to call him Rey, and he made me remember
the girl.

Or maybe it was the weather.

One of those wet springs in New York when the streets are under
water, and no collar can keep the wind-driven rain out. All through
March, when Marty came home with her show from Philadelphia, and
through most of April, Marty was in a bad mood. (Martine Adair, my
girl, who is almost twenty-eight and hasn't been a girl since long before I met her. She wasn't born with the name, or with anything else
that she cares about now, except, maybe, the ability to work hard and

long for what she wants. She wants to be an actress. No, to act, and she's good. Being good isn't always easy, not when you want to be good more than you want to be known.)

Her bad mood that April wasn't all the weather. She had trouble in her show. It came to be my trouble on another rainy Thursday in my small and gray bedroom.

"Go and kill him, Dan! Right now!"

"Knife, gun or my bare hand?"

She sat up in the bed. A small woman with long red hair, and big eyes, and the face of a young boy. It's the combination of the boy-face on the woman's body that kills the men, including me. That and her eagerness. She vibrates when she's sitting motionless. Her walk is a stride, and her anger is fury.

"He should be dead! He's got to die!"

"He will, honey. We all do."

"Spare me the damned philosophy, and do something."

"You want me to kill him for you? Just like that?"

"Passionately!" She lighted a cigarette, and looked down at me by the light of the flame. "I mean it."

She did mean it. I saw that in her eyes: a cold, gripping fury. She wanted Ricardo Vega dead, destroyed. And, no, she didn't mean it; not the normal, civilized Marty. Both, and at the same time. The complex drives of our needs.

"It's my role, I worked for it," she said. "Kurt says I'm good. He's the director. He says don't worry, but at the bank Vega's the whole show, and I know it. I fought him off in Philly, I don't want to fight anymore. I want him to stop. I don't want him in my bed."

"Can he get you fired?"

"Of course, if he made an issue. I don't think he will."

"But you're not sure, baby?"

"I'm sure, and I'm not sure."

"So maybe you'll say 'yes' in the end?"

"Does that make you sick?" Her eyes flashed down at me, because her anger had to go somewhere. Then she touched me, and turned her face away again. "The key word, Dan—'maybe.' That's how they work, the important lechers, the big-scorers who have to have what they're supposed to want—every girl they meet. He's attractive, they always are: handsome, strong, a public figure. He's exciting, and he's nice, you know? He won't get a girl fired, of course not, but . . . ? Why should a girl risk even that small maybe when it really might be pleasant? Bingo! It's easy when you know how, have the weapons."

Her voice was bitter in the gray evening light. She has fine breasts. I watched her breasts, and the long hair thick on her shoulders. That's me. She is someone else. She has her own needs.

"What do you want, Marty?"

"Go and tell him. He doesn't get me fired, and he doesn't get me! Hit him. Knock him down."

"With a club? One arm never won fair lady brawling."

"Scare him! You're a detective. Make him stop, Dan, before I say 'why not' because I'm scared of losing it all."

"All right, Marty," I said.

She dropped her cigarette into the ashtray, lay down close against me. She was warm. "Hurt him, Dan. Scare him. I worked so damned hard for the chance."

I knew how hard she'd worked for it, her first real role in a play, and after she had dressed and gone to her chorus rehearsal, I watched the rain for a while. When your woman asks you to act for her, you better act. At least, you had better if you wanted her friendly for the next month. I didn't want to meet Ricardo Vega on those terms. I didn't want to go to Vega so she would be nice to me later. It's not a noble reason—if it is honest, and the reason most men do favors for women, if the women want to face the way it is or not.

Yet I did want to meet Vega. I don't like men who trade on fear or hope; who scare or entice with their power to make or break dreams. So after a while I got up, dressed, and made myself think about that better reason for what I was doing. By the time I had my raincoat on I'd worked up a good anger. No one should ever have to live scared.

3

On my way out to get a taxi, I picked up a book I'd been reading. Vega was a producer, director, investor of his own money as well as an actor, and a book in my hand might help me get past the door easier.

The taxi dropped me at Lexington and Eighty-first Street. As I walked toward Vega's building the rain seemed to come down harder. An elegant marquee sheltered the glass-and-chrome doors of Vega's building, and a uniformed doorman stood inside the doors. I walked on. My book wouldn't help me get inside if I let the doorman announce me.

The basement service entrance bristled with signs that warned undesirables, but the door was unlocked. Those doors usually are, I've found. Detective experience has some uses. I stepped lightly in the basement in case a super was around, and went up into the lobby. I was lucky, the door opened into a wing of the lobby out of the doorman's sight. The elevators were self-service. Service wages are too high, so we live in an era of automation.

There were loud voices behind Vega's door when I rang. I had to ring again before the door was opened by a rawboned blond man with a lean, rough face and hungry eyes. His clothes—gray jacket, blue shirt and tie above the waist; chino levis and black Wellington boots below—and boyish but battered face gave the impression of a traveled twenty-year-old, but he was older: maybe twenty-eight. He looked uncertainly at my wet raincoat, black beret, book, and empty left sleeve as if he didn't know what he was supposed to do next.

I helped him out. "I want to see Vega."

"I don't know," he shrugged. "I'm waitin' myself."

"Fine," I said, and pushed in. "That makes two of us."

I was wrong. In the antechamber a skinny girl sat in a chrome chair as if waiting for execution, a thick play script held on her lap in both hands. In the living room, through an archway, there were three more people. The living room was mammoth, crammed with eclectic furniture that had cost twenty years' rent of my five cold-water rooms, and with the walls hidden by masses of magnificent paintings—all abstract, and all originals. The room of a prince of the world of art who breathed every minute in the rarefied air of the business of talent and genius, who knew everyone who was "doing" anything worth talking about.

Only one of the three in the living room was visible: a short, heavy, middle-aged man inside the archway. He was bald, gone to a pot, and his suit looked like it wrinkled over his flab one minute after he put it on. He was trying to look attentive and inconspicuous at the same time. That's a hard trick, and his flabby face glistened with sweat. The other two in the living room were only voices—a male and a female. I heard the female first.

"Hold the charm, Rey, okay? Just the score."

"No bugging me, Annie, please," the male voice said. It was a smooth, pleasant, very urbane voice. A tone of light banter didn't hide the confidence or power in the voice that told me, somehow, that the man behind the voice was handsome and much admired by women. There was a kind of creamy gallantry in the voice, but a weariness, too, and under it all a hint of cruder menace.

"Bug you?" the woman said, and I could hear the curl of her lip. "No woman bugs you, Rey."

"Come on, Anne, you're a big girl. It was fun, okay?"

"That's where we stand, Rey?"

There was a silence while the heavy man I could see went on sweating. I imagined the unseen pair staring at each other, their lips smiling, their eyes not.

"Don't try, Anne," the weary male said. "No trouble."

"Sure, you're a sweet guy. We had fun."

Now the iron surfaced in the man's urbane voice. Still smooth, still pleasant, but the gallantry was gone.

"Let me spell it out, Anne. I made no promises, no offers. You did what you wanted to do. What *you* wanted, no favors, right? It was nice, and maybe we do it again sometime."

There was that suspended silence again, the sense of the unseen man and woman watching each other, and then the woman spoke in a kind of tired voice. A sad voice.

"Okay, Rey. We better talk alone."

The man's voice, "Take Miss Terry to a taxi, George."

The sweating man stepped out of my sight, talking as he went, polite and deferential—a clerk. "Sure, Rey. Where you want to go, Miss Terry?"

The woman said, "We better talk in private, Rey."

"Get her out of here, George!"

George cajoled, "Please, Miss Terry, you know?"

"You want me to handle it, George?" the unseen man said.

It was the prince speaking: Where will you be tomorrow, George, if I have to do it myself? Why do I need you if you can't do the job for me?

"Okay, Miss Terry," George said, sharper. The changed voice of a man who fears to lose what he has.

George came into sight pushing the woman by one arm. She resisted, but under the heavy man's flab there was old muscle. When the woman saw the three of us waiting, she stopped her struggles. Her face turned neutral, and I saw that she was tall and much younger than her voice had sounded. I had a fast view of a pretty face, dark hair, full breasts and hips, and fine long thighs below a gray mini-mini skirt.

Then the door closed behind the young woman and George, and the urbane unseen man's voice spoke almost in my ear:

"Who the hell are you? What do they think I'm doing, casting a circus with one-armed freaks?"

His smooth voice was all stone now. I wasn't a woman.

2

HE WASN'T a big man, Ricardo Vega. About five-foot-ten, my height, but he looked taller. Slender and trim, good shoulders and no hips, he had to be my age, forty-five, but he didn't look that, either. He was very handsome, and he looked a lot younger. An aristocratic Latin face like some patrician young *hidalgo*: fine-boned yet masculine, with strong dark eyes. Dapper, yet there was a virile carelessness to his tailored blue jacket, gray slacks, low cordovan boots, and open blue shirt.

"What the devil are you supposed to be?" he said, that light, amused banter in his voice. "On your head, what is it? A black beret? One of Che Guevera's men? But you have to have a beard! Where's the beard?"

His hands, his whole body, moved with his voice in the flamboyance that was his strength. He was a great actor, a genius of the theater, few doubted that. From the moment he had walked out on a stage, only a few years rescued from a Cuban slum by a visiting American producer with an eye for talent, he had done what experts said couldn't be done. After Vega had done it, the same experts suddenly saw that Vega's way was the only way to do it. The true artist never finds an audience ready for him. He has to force his vision on the world, build his own audience. By now the whole country was his audience through his movies, but he was still at his best on stage in his own scripts, under his own direction. In the last few years he'd done his own productions. An institution—the Vega style.

"I'm not an actor, Vega," I said, aware that he had me psyched, on the defensive. "I'm a friend of Marty Adair."

"Marty?" he said. "A great girl, beautiful."

A change came over him the instant I mentioned Marty. I sensed that crude menace that seemed to be part of him, maybe from his old Cuban days, and that emerged, I guessed, when he was opposed. He reached out suddenly, and took the book from my hand.

"You wrote this? Of course, you're a writer!"

"No," I said. It was *Portnoy's Complaint*. A joke on me.

"You're not Philip Roth? That's too bad."

His apologetic grin was full of mock sadness at my failure to be "somebody," to have talent. His whole body seemed to droop in sympathy for me. He winked at his audience. The skinny girl smiled uneasily, and clutched her script. The blond man laughed. Never debate an actor, they have the weapons.

"My name's Fortune, Vega," I said. My only defense was a blunt attack. "Marty's my woman. She worked for her job, she's going to keep it."

"Why not, man?" he said lightly, his eyes not light, deciding how he could slap me down hardest. "Fortune? Wait, now, Marty talked some. Dan Fortune, sure, the gumshoe! A detective, now that's impressive."

I said, "You want me to make it plain, Vega?"

"Plain? Sure, go ahead, make it plain."

"Stop bothering Marty, and don't try—"

He hit me good. A faint drop of his right shoulder, and a sucker right hand lead, and I was on the floor with an ache in my chin. I'm no fighter, and while I was getting up I had time to remember that in his long-ago Cuban days he had been. It looked like he kept in shape and practice. I got up, but I needed a chair to hold onto for a time. I saw pretty colors.

That mocking weariness was in his voice. "Don't come here and warn me, Fortune. You want to keep Marty, you work to keep her, okay? That's the game. If I'm too much for you to handle, that's too bad. You over there," he looked at the blond man, "what's your name?"

The blond man jumped a foot. "Me, Mr. Vega? Rick McBride."

"My friends call me Rey," Vega said, eyeing the blond McBride. "We'll have to get rid of that 'Rick' name; those dream-boy tags are out these days. Something ethnic, maybe, like Sean. Now throw this idiot out, and we'll talk."

"Me?" McBride said, his mouth open.

My head was clear. I didn't need the chair now, but I was less match for McBride than for Vega. McBride's face had those marks of a rough youth, and his eyes were hungry on me.

"You," Vega said. "I want to see how you move. He's trespassing; you can hit him."

McBride looked everywhere except at me. He was working up an anger. I put my hand into my raincoat pocket, mimed a pistol. A useless trick against the experienced, but McBride and Vega weren't used to guns. They knew I was a detective, they didn't know I don't often carry a gun, and they would expect a weapon from a one-armed man. In our suddenly violent world guns have come to be common. Few normal men will take the chance. They didn't.

"Remember you're no king to me, Vega," I said.

I backed out, gunman style. Hitting a one-armed man wasn't going to enhance Vega's image. I'd won the face-off on points. It was there in the way the skinny girl watched me, not Vega. I didn't think she was going to have much luck with whatever she wanted from Vega. Face means a lot to men like him.

I should have kept that in mind, but when I walked out of the lobby, the wrinkled man, George, and the girl Vega had thrown out of his apartment were standing out in the wet night beyond the service alley. The rain was coming hard, and George had no coat, but the girl was talking and he was listening. I slipped into the alley to see what I could hear.

The rain drummed on garbage cans, and I couldn't hear what the girl was saying. I tried too hard. The arm was around my neck, squeezing my throat, before I heard a step. He dragged me back down the alley. I got a foot against a wall and heaved backward. We went down in a river of water with me on top. His arm came loose. I got my chin under the arm, and bit hard. He howled. I broke free, and scrambled up.

All my fight did me no good; he was the stronger man. I started to run, but my feet slipped, and a violent blow on my back made me gasp. I half-turned and took a punch that numbed my lone arm. The next two punches were more accurate. I went down flat in the alley, my nose and mouth bleeding.

"Mr. Vega says don't bother him."

It was the blond, McBride. He leaned and slapped my face twice, hard. It hurt. My mind thought about his name. Would he decide on Sean? My foot kicked him in the belly. He kicked me in the ribs, bent and hit me in the face with a fist, kicked me again, and again. The girl Vega had thrown out before me saved me from the hospital or worse.

"Hey! You dirty—! Police!"

McBride ran for the building. After all, he was just a roustabout aspiring to be an actor. That's what I figured he was. I sat up and tested for damage. Blood and bruises, no more. The girl still stood at the open end of the alley. I limped out to her.

"Thanks," I said. "I'll ache, but I'll heal."

Close, she was less pretty but more opulent. Her face was long and bony, with the tired look that doesn't come from worry or conflict, but from plain too much work and not enough sleep. Her eyes were too bright, feverish, as if she lived on energy alone. But her full body was really beautiful. I found I envied Ricardo Vega. For this girl in bed, even I might—?

I said, "Vega doesn't like you, either."

"You better fade out, Gunner."

Her voice still had the quality I had heard up in Ricardo Vega's living room—direct, a little hard, and older than her years. A voice of bone, not sugar.

"We could help each other out," I said.

"I don't guess so. Mind your own henhouse."

I heard a regional sound in her voice, far from New York.

"I need a weapon," I said. "Two hit harder than one."

She smiled at that. A nice smile. Not innocent or eager, but friend-ly. She reached out and touched my bruised face. When a woman has known few men, she will usually flinch from physical touch, will make a big thing of it. This girl had been with many men, her touch firm and matter-of-fact. Her fingers came away bloody. She looked at the blood.

"I don't need losers, Gunner. Bring me the winner."

"He's a bastard, Miss Terry."

"And a genius. You know it. If you want the theater, he's where the action is. The power, Gunner."

"What is he as a man?"

"Power there, too, Gunner. You believe it."

"I believe a brush-off when I hear one."

She seemed to think about that, about the brush-off, and after a time she sighed. "I really dig the guy, too, except he'll never be sure enough to relax. Too bad."

She blinked in the rain. For an instant I was aware of a real sense of loss about her. Then she began to walk away without looking at me again. "Go sniff around your own bird, Gunner."

Her walk was a stride like Marty's. After a few seconds, I sloshed behind her toward my subway. She turned at Lexington, and when I reached the corner, I saw her go into a cafeteria up the block. Under the conditions, that seemed strange to me. She wasn't the type of girl who ate in cafeterias. Maybe it was only the bloodhound habit, but I followed. Through the cafeteria window I saw her carry two cups of coffee to a table, and look at her watch. I waited in the rain.

A tall, pale, skinny man appeared and walked toward her table. He had a stoop, and a kind of shuffle as if his feet hurt. His enormous hands stuck out of short topcoat sleeves. The coat was too small, and shabby, and his pants were work pants. He wore work boots. He had a gaunt face and sunken eyes, but I guessed that he was only in his early forties. The early forties of a man who'd lived a long and hard life.

He sat down at the girl's table, his coat still on. She pushed a cup to him. They sat without speaking. When he had finished his coffee, he just stared at her. She took one of his big hands. Her face was gentle, her eyes soft. His reaction surprised me—he hung his head, looked at the floor. I could see the pressure as she squeezed his big hand. She talked for some minutes, smiling almost sadly, as if the two of them were alone in the cheap cafeteria. Then she patted his hand.

His gaunt head jerked up. For the first time he spoke, and I saw a sharp exchange between them. It was over in seconds. He stood up slowly, reluctant. She nodded to the door. At that he turned and walked away. I watched him come out and go north. He didn't look back. Inside, she went to the telephone. She returned to the table with another cup of coffee. I had a quick hunch, and moved into a doorway next to the cafeteria from where I could look out at intervals.

When I saw them they were already around the corner and near me in the rain. Ricardo Vega, and another man. I shrank back, and hoped the other man wasn't Rick McBride, or Sean, and, if it was, I hoped even more that he wouldn't spot me.

It wasn't McBride, it was the heavy man, George, and he didn't spot me. But he took up my old post outside the cafeteria window. Vega went inside. I didn't have to see Vega to know where he went inside the cafeteria, and with George outside I wasn't going to see anything more. All I would do was risk more lumps, and no matter who the gaunt man had been, I didn't see anything in it all to help my problem.

I slipped carefully from the doorway, but George had no interest in me or anything else outside that cafeteria. I took the subway downtown, and stopped in on Doc Silverman. He patched my cuts, felt my face bones, clucked over my bruises, and sent me home. My five cold rooms were a bleak welcome. After Vega's place they looked like a rural railroad waiting room. In Europe people are used to coming home to cold rooms, to moving around in coats until the heat takes hold. Americans expect cozy heat, and a frigid apartment is depressing.

I was depressed enough anyway. Bruises aside, I hadn't done much for Marty. I felt no better when she arrived about 2:00 A.M., even though my rooms were warm, and a good movie was on TV. She saw my band-aids and bruises.

"Dan, who? Vega? No!"

"Did he bother you again tonight, Mart?"

"I didn't see him; they didn't rehearse my scene. The understudies worked separate. What happened?"

I told her blow for blow, verbal and physical. "I don't think I did much good, baby."

"He knows I'm not alone now, Dan."

"You think that'll help?"

"He likes the easy chase, the sitting pigeon, no fuss," she said, kissed me. "You know, I love you a whole lot."

Reason number one for going to Ricardo Vega had worked fine. She was nice to me the rest of that night. I liked it, but it made me uneasy. Gratitude is a bad base for passion. No woman loves a man long because she's grateful.

So, after she was asleep, I lay in the dark and tried to think that Vega would lay off Marty because of me.

3

I SHOULD have known better. For a week it did seem possible, but men like Ricardo Vega don't change in a week. Marty was ready to cry; except that Marty doesn't cry; she swears.

"Damn, damn, damn! He's got that 'business manager' of his, George Lehman, hinting that the boss is worried, maybe I lack spark, fire! There ought to be more 'life' in my scene!"

The first week, Vega was just busy. The man aside, he was a great actor, had written the show, his own money was in it, and when there was an artistic purpose to serve, he served it first. The second week he was the king again.

"King of toads!" Marty said. Her work meant too much to her. "He squats on his pad, croaks his power, and licks out that sticky tongue to snare all the flies."

I was helpless, and that's a hell of a feeling. I had no power to pressure Ricardo Vega, and I couldn't fight him physically. A gun was no threat. He would be sure by now that I wasn't going to use a gun. Yet I had to do something, and I thought a lot about Ricardo Vega the second week. That was why I spotted the girl's name in the newspaper. In *The Daily News*. The story wasn't in *The Times*, of course. I think it was only the picture that even got it into *The News*. *The News* likes pictures of pretty girls.

I don't often read *The News*, but in my one-window office that Monday morning I had nothing to do but think about Ricardo Vega. It was a sunny spring day at last. I wanted to relax and enjoy the day over some beers, or maybe I needed a friend to talk to—a real friend. Only Joe Harris fitted that need—one friend, not counting Marty; the fate of a man who belongs nowhere. But Joe wouldn't be on duty at Black's Tavern until noon. I had an hour, so I read *The News*.

The picture of the big girl in the small bikini stopped me on page four:

NUDE ACTRESS VANISHES

Anne Terry, 22, actress and model, who made headlines when she appeared nude for a whole act in a banned production at The New Player's Theater, was reported missing late last night. The disappearance of the curvy actress was reported by her sister, Sarah Wiggen, of 29 West Seventy-sixth Street, who told police her sex-pot sister vanished last Thursday from her West Tenth Street apartment.

Her partner in New Player's Theater, Theodore Marshall, 26, questioned by police, denied any knowledge of her whereabouts. Marshall said he could think of no reason for the beauty to have vanished. Police are investigating.

There was no mention of Ricardo Vega, but it was the girl in the rain all right. Her name brought the night back to me, "Go sniff around your own bird, Gunner." A girl who had wanted to talk to Vega alone. Who had been thrown out, had talked to the bald man, George, who had then called, and Vega had come to her. A brush-off, a summons, and now a disappearance. It was worth a look. I had liked Anne Terry, she had helped me.

The noble detective. All ready to connect Ricardo Vega to one missing girl in the hundreds he had dropped. With his power and money, and her obvious background? A "free" girl, who had to know fifty men more desperate than Vega; and a rich man who could pay off a dozen girls, one way or the other. After over two weeks, I was suspicious of foul play by Ricardo Vega? When his name wasn't in the story, and *The News* a paper that would jump with joy at even a hint of the great man?

Not to help the girl, no. A straw. A chance to cause Vega trouble. There was a connection, if slim, and maybe I could at least bruise Vega. Then, anything was possible. Famous men do make mistakes.

I took a taxi to the West Seventy-sixth Street address of the sister, Sarah Wiggen. The day was crisp, the trees in the park budding with new, bright green that didn't last long in New York. Somehow, that made me think of the missing girl, Anne Terry, who must have been green and bright once, but who had long lost it when I had talked to her in the rain. Lost it at the age of twenty-two.

Sarah Wiggen had never had it. The sister opened her door to my ring, and maybe she had been green once, but she had never been bright—alive bright, I mean, not intelligent bright.

"Yes?" she said, stared at my empty sleeve.

Maybe she was intelligent, I couldn't say, but I could guess that she had always been drab, earthbound. She looked enough like her sister to prove the relation, but where Anne Terry had worn gray and looked gaudy, Sarah Wiggen wore red and looked gray. Not that she wasn't pretty, and almost as well filled out, but the classic bones of her sister were missing, and something more—the spark, the verve, the intangible that makes men turn.

"Miss Wiggen? Can I talk to you about your sister?"

"Anne?" Her tone could have been eagerness—or surprise. Her voice lacked the bone, but it had the same regional accent. "You know where she is? Come in."

Moving, she looked more like her sister. It gave her animation. The apartment couldn't move, and it lay there, cheap and dull. The colors seemed to cancel each other out, and there was no eye for style. It wasn't eclectic, it was simply polyglot, mismatched, and there wasn't much of it. A bare apartment, but not empty. A man stood up.

"Did I hear that Anne has been found?" he said.

A florid-faced man of medium height, but topping my 160 pounds by a good fifty. He didn't look fat, just thick, like a broad tree trunk. Part of that effect was his clothes: brown tweed jacket with leather elbow patches; soft, checked shirt; green wool tie; pin-stripe flannel pants that belonged to a suit; good brown shoes badly run over at the heel.

"No," I said, "I want to help you find her. My name's Dan Fortune, I'm a detective."

"A police detective?" the florid man asked.

"Private. I met Anne a few weeks ago at Ricardo Vega's apartment. I'd like to help if you'll let me."

"Vega?" the man said, glanced at Sarah Wiggen. "Perhaps he could help you, Sarah."

"I can't pay a detective," she said.

"I don't want pay. On my own."

"You have some personal angle?" the man said.

"Anne helped me once, and I don't like Ricardo Vega. He could be involved. I want to find out. That's straight."

"It is," the man said.

He went to Sarah Wiggen, put his arm around her shoulders.

"Why not let him try, Sarah? He could help."

He could have been her father, but he didn't act fatherly. Maybe fifty years old, less. Probably the same age, nearly, as Ricardo Vega—but this man looked almost fifty, and Vega looked barely thirty. (It's partly a matter of will, of desire. Some men look forty at twenty-five: mature, responsible, proper. They want to look mature; they are in the main stream—firm fathers, solid husbands, mature in business. Other men look boyish, immature, at forty. Men out of the main stream who value personal youth and their individual ego. A matter of a man's self-image.)

"If he wants to, all right," Sarah Wiggen agreed.

"Give me a dollar to make it legal," I said. "You're my client."

She found a dollar in her handbag, and gave it to me.

"Good," I said, and turned to the man. "Now why did Ricardo Vega's name mean something to you? Mr.—?"

"Emory Foster," the florid man said.

"You know Anne Terry?" I asked him.

"No, I never met her," he said, "and Vega means nothing to me. It's Sarah he has meaning for."

"What meaning?" I said to the sister. "His name wasn't in the story in the newspaper."

"It will be," Emory Foster said. "She just told the police."

"Why did you wait?" I asked the girl.

"I didn't list all the names of the men Anne knew," she said. "Only Ted Marshall, because he was her current boy friend. I don't even know all her men."

Emory Foster said, "I told her to tell the police all she knew. Especially about Ricardo Vega."

"What does she know about Vega?"

"That Anne was in his acting class," Sarah Wiggen said, "and that they . . . they played around."

"Vega plays around with a lot of girls."

"I guess he does."

I waited. "That's all? No trouble with Vega?"

"I don't know. We're not close, Mr. Fortune. I don't see her much. We live different, and we don't talk to each other that often."

"Then how do you know she's missing?"

"I talked to her Thursday," she said. "She called to ask me to go down home with her. We haven't been home in four years, at least I haven't, but I didn't want to go with her. I called her Friday morning to tell her. She didn't answer. She's always home on Friday mornings. Ted Marshall gets Fridays off, and they work. She's never home on weekends, so I didn't think too much about Friday until Sunday. She was supposed to call me, definitely, on Sunday evening to get my answer about going down home. When she didn't call, I went down to her place."

"It worried you that much? Just not calling once?"

"Anne always does what she says she'll do. Always," Sarah Wiggen said. "The super had to let me into her place. I saw that she hadn't been home since at least early Friday. The place was all neat, untouched. Anne always straightens on Thursdays for Ted coming on Friday. She'd never clean on a weekend. To me that meant that she hadn't been home since maybe Thursday evening. I called Ted Marshall. He said when he went on Friday morning, she hadn't been home. She hadn't told him she'd be away. So when she still wasn't home late Sunday night, I went to the police."

"That was pretty quick, wasn't it?" I said.

Emory Foster said, "Her being missing Friday makes this weekend different. She didn't tell Marshall she'd miss their regular meeting on Friday morning, and she expected to be at home on Sunday evening. Sarah tells me Anne is very orderly. And she still isn't at home, is she?"

I thought about it. "Where is 'down home,' Sarah?"

"North Carolina, a dirt farm. She's not there, I called the general store, talked to my Ma."

"Which one of you changed the name?"

"Anne. She married at fourteen," she said, almost bitterly. "Annie May Terrell. She shortened it for acting."

"What's her number on Tenth Street? You have no key?"

"She never gave me a key. Number 110, apartment four."

"I'll see what I can find," I said.

Neither of them said any more, and both of them stood as if they were waiting for me to leave before they moved. That made me wonder, but not as much as the timing of Sarah Wiggen's report to the police. It had been fast, no matter what they said.

4

THE BUILDING at 110 West Tenth Street was in the part of Greenwich Village taken over years ago by well-paid fringe artists—editors, copy-writers, commercial artists, theater producers, designers, professors. People who had once wanted to be real artists, free livers, and who came to live where others were still trying. But they had jobs and children, needed to be clean and safe. The aspiring or stubborn real artists were careless, dirty, and not always safe, so were driven out by those who had come to love them. Only the few artists who had been highly successful could stay. The rest had to find lower rents on less careful streets, evicted by those who wanted the name of artist, but who, in the end, feared the game.

The street was clean, tree-lined and expensive, and Anne Terry's brownstone building silent in the early afternoon. A ring got no response. I used my rectangle of stiff plastic to open the vestibule door, and the ninth key on my ring of master keys opened the apartment door. It was the top floor; flooded with sun, and empty.

There were two rooms and a kitchenette, laid out much like Sarah Wiggen's apartment, and with not much more furniture, but there the resemblance ended. The difference, as with the sisters themselves, summed up in a few words —spark, verve, style, the in-tangible. Everything blended, yet there was nothing "arranged" about the place. All casual, even careless, and, yes, warm. I had not ex-pected a warm apartment—"I don't need losers, Gunner. Bring me the winner."

I began work with the closets. Those in the bedroom held only fe-male clothes, and not as many as I expected. Few outfits for a woman, especially a theater woman—one or two good ensembles for each occasion, no waste, like a general planning a battle. In the living room closet there was a man's green tartan jacket, a pair of gray slacks. The jacket had a name strip sewn to the collar: Theodore Marshall.

He was her partner, he came here often, it told me nothing. Her bedroom chest-of-drawers did. There were four shirts still in laundry wrappers; three pairs of socks, size thirteen; brief undershorts; two ties; an electric razor, male; all but the ties and razor with the same sewn name strip: Theodore Marshall. So Ted Marshall was more than her partner: surprise!

The chest-of-drawers yielded another less than surprising find. A single cuff link initialed: R.V., and a green tie figured in gold with crowns and tiny initials: R.V. At least it was solid evidence that Ricardo Vega had known her well.

I found nothing under cushions, under furniture, under the big bed, under the rugs, in the corners, or in the table drawers. Nothing on shelves, on the mantelpiece, or in the various vases and decorative boxes. The apartment had been cleaned, and some time ago by the layer of grit undisturbed inside the one open window. The window confirmed that Anne Terry had not expected to be away long —in New York no one leaves a window open if they plan to be away long.

I finished with the one odd feature of the apartment: an old desk, and a cardboard filing cabinet, in a corner behind a screen. The file held a folder of the lease and rent receipts; another of time-payment contracts for the TV, clothes, some furniture; and a thick folder labeled: New Player's Theater. No bankbooks and no tax records, which surprised me—she was a neat, efficient girl.

I went through The New Player's Theater folder. It showed the theater to be in the red—usual for an Off-Broadway venture. But it wasn't too far into the red; it had been well-managed. Programs proved that it was a serious theater, producing the difficult work of avant-garde playwrights, as well as the work of pseudo-avantists who dealt in shock-and-snicker. The shockers had run longer, naturally, but none of the plays had run long.

The bulk of the file was Projected Plans, and they were ambitious. The New Player's had been planning for better quarters. Profit-and-loss, rentals, and the needed capital had been worked out for all theaters. Plans for new productions were detailed: ambitious productions, daring. Hard work had gone into the planning, not just dazzling verbal dreams over booze, and it added to busy work for a future, a real future. Bold, needing money, but not the work of a girl who wanted to vanish.

The desk, too, was neat, the top pigeonholes empty except for the usual paid bills, and a day-calendar book. The datebook explained that overworked, underslept face I had seen in the rain. Days began early, ended late: The New Player's; auditions for paying shows; a modeling job, regular, and a host of irregular jobs like artist's model, photographer's model, product demonstrator, even typist. At night there were classes, and nameless appointments. There were sparse weeks, almost blank pages, but no page totally blank —always The New Player's.

The top drawer explained her nights. A litter of matchbooks, stirring rods, coasters, all from night clubs, cafés, hotels; male business cards, many with lip prints. Par for the course again; a girl with looks and ambitions surviving in New York. I didn't envy the police if she were really missing, and if her closer friends knew nothing. A life of casual encounters, one-night stands. A busy fly in a world of toads? Caught at last? Except, I saw Anne Terry as more of a hornet, with sting.

The bankbooks were in a bottom drawer. A savings account with nothing: $197. A checking account, the stubs showing no pattern of deposit except the weekly modeling check, and showing near zero too often—saved by a sudden deposit, sometimes good, sometimes not. The weekly paycheck from the regular job interested me. Most companies like to pay monthly, or bi-weekly at most. It had to be an arrangement she had wanted.

The canceled checks themselves seemed uninteresting at first: mostly bills from the payees, and regular ones to The New

Player's—she was a real owner, not a decoration for Ted Marshall. But after I had stacked them, I had a small pile of checks made out to *cash*. Normal, except that there was a pattern. Almost all the cash-checks were for the same amount, fifty dollars, and almost all were dated on Fridays. I checked the calendar.

I sat back and stared at the cash-checks. She was neat, but was anyone that regular in her kind of life? It could be nothing, but—? There were missing Fridays, yes, a few drawn on Thursdays, but in general the uniformity of day and amount was too much coincidence. In a hectic life, did a girl always run out of cash on Friday? And could she always need exactly fifty dollars? All right, a special need; regular, routine. What? Blackmail? Fifty dollars? A regular contribution? But in cash, so she wasn't sending it home, or anywhere by mail.

I was still mulling it, turning it over and considering all angles, when the doorbell rang. I jumped a foot in the chair, then had a surge of something like joy. Anne Terry, coming home? I was coming to like the girl, and not in the way Ricardo Vega liked girls. I was also losing my grip. Would a girl ring her own doorbell?

I was out of the chair. The police? They would have been here to check that she was really gone, but, from the look of the place, they hadn't searched much. She had not been gone long enough to make them take it seriously at first—off on a binge, ninety-nine percent. But they would have another, closer, look if she didn't turn up. So I had my leg over the window sill to the fire escape when the door was tried and given a violent kick.

I came back inside, and trotted lightly to the door. The police don't kick in doors of empty apartments; they get the super to open up. I slid behind where the door would open as a second good kick cracked the lock. The third kick would do it. It did. The door flew open and all the way back to me. I took a bash on the knuckles, but held the door from swinging back out.

The man stumbled into the room, off balance. I got one quick look at him as he went by the crack between door and frame. The blond again—Rick, or Sean, McBride. Vega's new volunteer helper—for friendship. I stayed where I was, out of sight, my lone hand ready in a fist if he closed the door. He didn't, he was that much an amateur, and that nervous. He hurried for the bedroom. When I heard a drawer open, I went after him, picking up a handy, large, but not too heavy vase on the way.

He was bent over a drawer in the bedroom, his back to me. I wanted to ask him what he was up to, but it's not often that easy. I had no gun, and I didn't expect he was going to tell much without heavy pressure. I did the next best thing. I whacked him good with the vase. Not too good, just enough. It was a pleasure. He collapsed in a heap. I got out of there fast.

I was out the door, and one flight down, when I heard them coming up. Two men who had not rung the girl's doorbell, and a pair of lighter feet coming behind them. I beat it back up. McBride was moving inside already, with groans. I made the stairs up to the roof, hidden from Anne Terry's doorway. The two men had eyes only for the open door. I heard them go in. There was a scuffle, and voices.

"Who are you? What's the story?"

"Someone hit me!" McBride's outraged voice. The two newcomers had to be the police, and McBride wasn't worried about them yet, only about me. He had a lot to learn.

"Breaking-and-entering, mister."

"Who are you? We got the super for a witness."

"You broke that vase? Looking for what? Jewels?"

"Where's the girl?"

McBride, "I don't know, I come to see her. A friend, like."

"Your name, mister!"

"Sean McBride."

A rebirth for Rick McBride! Maybe a star was being born.

"You busted that door? Why?"

"It was open, you know? Like, I told you I'm a friend. The door was open, so I come in. Someone hit me. Maybe it was you two, yeh!"

I revised my estimate of Rick, no, Sean McBride. He wasn't dumb, and he thought fast under pressure. It was a good story if he stuck to it. They couldn't prove it was false, he wasn't a criminal, he did know Anne Terry more or less, he had kept Ricardo Vega out of it, and he hinted at a possible charge of police brutality. Reasonable doubt all the way.

I left by way of the roof. They would hammer him more, take him to precinct, let him sweat, but they would get no more from him now that he had his story. He had been around, and he had more brains than I had guessed.

I went down to the street through another building. I wondered just how well McBride had known Anne Terry.

5

I WALKED down Fifth Avenue, and across Washington Square, among the spring hordes of a sunny Village afternoon. The well-dressed men and their women, the outsiders from "real" life, wandered giggling and pointing, having one hell of a time gawking at the bizarre flora and fauna of this year's Village population. The bright-colored local birds-of-passage themselves—all shapes, sexes and skins, each in the plumage of his choice—stared at no one and nothing, all going somewhere, intent on their purpose. That makes you wonder.

On Third Street The New Player's Theater was tucked between an open pizza stand and a psychedelic poetry-reading club. A tiny marquee, with pictures of the players in action outside. There was a padlock on the inner doors. A sign indicated that tickets for the next production wouldn't go on sale for three weeks. The photos outside were from an earlier production.

Anne Terry was in most of the photos, and I had another view of her: the actress. Good or bad I couldn't know from the pictures, but they told me one thing—Anne Terry wasn't just a pretty face with her good side to the camera, or her breasts stuck into your eye. She had been caught in action; neck cords stretched like ropes, mouth twisted, body in powerful motion. An intensity that came over even in still shots. Intense: the one word I could fit to all I had seen of her so far, and I didn't see her abandoning all she was doing. But if she had chucked it all, that intensity would make it hard to find her.

There was a portrait of Theodore Marshall, and he was easy to spot in the action shots. Intense wasn't a word for Marshall. Tall, slender, handsome in a juvenile way, with a brooding face and thick, black hair. No actor—posed, stiff, mugging emotion; all surface, all conscious attitude, the eyes uninvolved and even a little scared. Maybe a lover of theater, but no actor. Yet the man I had to find next. The first drugstore gave me his address from the telephone book.

It was only a few blocks away across Sixth Avenue. A red brick apartment house. The best, semi-new building on a block of tenement brownstones. It had gone to seed, the bare lobby shabby with streaks on the stone floor where a wet mop had been swished around in a feeble show of cleaning. A solid, middle-class New York apartment house, neither good nor slum: respectable. Theodore Marshall lived on the fifth floor. I rode up.

An older woman answered my ring. "Yes?"

She was small and motherly, thickened by years of routine daily round in a simple, accepted world. She was dressed now in a suit, on her way out, and her hair was dyed dark. She looked at my missing arm.

"Mr. Theodore Marshall?" I asked.

"Theodore?" She paused. "Is it about his theater?"

"About Anne Terry."

"Anne? Well, come in then."

Brisk, she led me into a square living room that looked as if it had been there a long time. Clean and pleasant, but with the dusty feeling that comes from age, wear and little change. She sat down, perched on a couch with her handbag on her lap.

"Well, tell me," she said. "You've found her? Where was the silly girl? You're police?"

She made me think of Ricardo Vega again, of his age. Five, maybe ten years older, the woman looked like Vega's mother. The will inside a person again. This woman content, even insistent, to be old and comfortable like the heavy, styleless furniture of the room. Only the dyed hair struck a false note. From the hair, and the outdoor suit, I judged she worked.

"A private detective," I said. "We haven't found Anne as far as I know."

"Private detective? Then you've come to ask Theodore more questions? I assure you my son told all he knew."

"People remember later," I said. "New questions."

I had the feeling of being interrogated, screened before I could see some dignitary. My business was being analyzed, and found not sufficiently urgent.

"He's tried to remember anything. We're both worried, of course. Perhaps if you came back later?"

"Time could be important, Mrs. Marshall."

She accepted the name. So Theodore Marshall lived with his mother. It didn't fit my image of him, but, then, what image could I have yet? All his clothes at Anne Terry's apartment—a home away from Mother? The rent right in both places?

"But he's asleep, you see?" Mrs. Marshall said. "He's hardly slept since he heard about Anne. He had an accident last week, quite serious. Now I must go to work."

I didn't want to push too hard, but, "If I could—"

An inner door opened in the kitchen beyond the living room where the windows overlooked a rear courtyard and the walls of tenements across the yards. Theodore Marshall came out, his fingers automatically straightening his thick hair. In person he was taller and thinner. He wore narrow black slacks custom-made to his slim hips, a silky blue-and-white cotton shirt Ricardo Vega would admire, a sky-blue silk tie, and cuff links of sky-blue stones. A man who liked good clothes— so much that he napped in them. Mrs. Marshall's eyes showed that for Theodore Marshall admiration began at home. Maybe only love.

"I heard, Ma," he said. He had a soft, pleasant voice, eager now. "You're a private eye? Can you find Anne? I mean, like, you were hired? Mr.—?"

"Dan Fortune. Sarah Wiggen hired me."

Surprise arched his pale face. He had an unhealthy pallor, and his eyes up close were very pale hazel—the impression of dark eyes coming from sunken eye sockets with dark circles. I had seen faces like his on gamblers who worked tensely in smoky rooms far from the sunlight, and who lay awake nights full of schemes. Like Anne Terry, Marshall had the look of a man who burned his candle at all ends. At least from what I could see of his normal face. I couldn't see too much. One eye was badly bruised and puffed almost shut. His lips were split, swollen. His nose looked thick and scabbed, and a bandage covered his left ear and part of his cheek. There was a thickness under the silky shirt that had to be bandaged ribs. He saw me staring.

"Stupid trick," he said wryly. "Doing the pipe lights at the theater. Ladder went over, I landed off the stage in the pit. Damn near a hospital job."

"You're surprised Sarah Wiggen hired me?"

"Sure as hell am. Not that it isn't damned sweet of Sarah, but, Christ, I didn't figure she'd care that much."

"Please, Theodore," Mrs. Marshall said.

He grinned, punched her lightly on the arm. "Come on, Ma, I'm a big boy."

She smiled like a girl. She liked it, her boy's buddy charm. I realized that it was his swearing she was clucking over, and that it was a standard game with them. They seemed to have a nice relationship. I wondered what Mr. Marshall had been like—dull and solid, probably, a quiet man.

"Sarah and Anne didn't get along?" I asked. Sarah Wiggen had hinted at the same thing, but had at least implied that the aloofness was all on Anne's side.

"Well," Marshall grinned, even blushed, "Sarah and me, I, we had a thing for a while. Before I met Anne, you know? We were in the same class a while, me and Sarah. Scene class."

"Sarah's an actress, too?"

"Was, not now. Quit it. Got some mother-hen job in some kind of residence hall for females."

"You and Sarah?" I said. "Then Anne came along?"

"Bingo, that's it. We had the same ideas, you know?"

His voice, still soft and pleasant, jerked and jumped like a spastic. Nervous: voice and body. His strange, light eyes were hard to really see, elusive. I saw in them, vaguely, that same self-awareness I had seen in the action pictures of him at the theater, a small fear that seemed part of him. Not for now, always; as if he lived every day a little afraid. I remembered a very young second mate on a Liberty ship during the war whose eyes had been like that when we entered the war zone. Not afraid of the submarines in themselves, but afraid every day that something would happen to the skipper and first mate, leaving him. A man in over his head on nerve he didn't really have.

"You're nervous," I said. "Worried about Anne?"

"That," he said, nodded. "Maybe more worried without her, you know? She's the force. Without her, what do I do? What if she's cut out, ditched the theater and all?"

"You know any reasons she would ditch it?"

"Not a one."

"Nothing? Friends, plans, troubles?"

"Who knows, you know? I went over on Friday like usual. She wasn't home. No word before or since. I never see her on weekends, of course. That's her time with the big sports, money work. Sarah says she talked about going down home, but not to me she didn't."

"You had big plans for your theater," I said. "Plans that cost money. Could that be part of her disappearance?"

"Plans? Hell, we're not even sure of the next show."

Mrs. Marshall objected, "Perhaps you didn't have big plans, Theodore, but I know Anne did. Why, I've heard her talking about them here. It worried me for you. She's too ambitious."

"Knock it off, Ma," Marshall said. His voice was curt. "Pipe dreams; pie-in-the-sky. Anne and her big dreams. All fog, you know?"

"Dreams can be trouble," I said. "Money and influence, is that what she was after?"

Marshall nodded. Mrs. Marshall wasn't even listening to me. Her eyes were for her boy.

"She's too old for you, Theodore," she said.

His pale eyes looked to the ceiling for help. "For Christ sake, Ma, I'm four years older than Anne."

"She's a mature woman. You're still a boy," she said.

"That's swell, thanks. A boy who lives off his mother, right? Go to work for me, Ma. Work your ass off!"

She flinched, but her voice was calm. "That's hardly called for in front of a stranger." She looked at me. "Theodore doesn't like me to work, especially not at night. I'm not fond of it, but the theater is demanding. He works much too hard, really. He has his odd-hour job, though I'm against that. He shouldn't waste time on money work without future. Still, the job pays for his clothes, and appearance is vital in the theater. Of course, I wish Theodore wanted a more solid career, but a career is useless if it isn't what a man wants. Theodore must have his chance, and you get nowhere with half measures. Now is the time he has to think only of his goal. I'm really quite selfish, you see. Investing for my old age when he's rich."

Her smile was a little mocking of herself. A mother who was justifying her son, but who was also pushing him to face his own goals more seriously. Forcing him to really think of the theater, and not of the girls, the good times, the swagger of being a man of the theater. Trying to make a man of a boy, and what the hell else should a mother do?

Ted Marshall laughed. "A real selfish old hard nut, yes she is." He sat on the arm of the couch, put his arm around her. "Sorry, Ma, you know? I'll get rich for you. Okay?"

"You're all blarney, Theodore," she said, smiled up at him. "Now I must go to work. Try to get some sleep, Theodore." And to me, "Not too long, Mr. Fortune, please."

She got up only a little slowly, and went out without waiting for an answer. I heard her walking toward the elevator. Ted Marshall stared at the closed door.

"I do live on her. Thanks, Ma, maybe you can take it easy when you're a hundred. Damn, I will make it up to her. Now all my loot is for the theater, the big front."

"Where do you work?"

"Nat Brown, the agent. Four days 'til three."

31

"Tell me about Ricardo Vega."

"Vega? What about Vega?"

"Anne was having an affair with him, right?"

"Not that I know. She's in his class, that's all."

"You're a boyfriend?"

"We make it. No strings, she got to live, and our theater needs money. I never see her weekends, I don't ask about it."

"You don't know of any trouble with Vega?"

"Trouble? No, I don't."

I thought. "She said to me once that Vega was the power, the action. She wanted to talk to him about something private. Did she ever talk about him backing your theater, helping, or maybe about getting money from him?"

"No," he said. "You know Anne?"

"A battlefield meeting, once," I said.

He puzzled me. Was he so naive, or jealous, that she hadn't told him? Because if he knew about Vega, why hide it? If he had nothing to do with her disappearance, he should want Vega's possible role investigated. If he was part of whatever had happened to her, if anything, why not jump at the chance to put suspicion on Ricardo Vega? He wasn't putting suspicion on anyone.

"Hell," he said, "she'll come back soon, you see."

"Come back? You know she's gone somewhere?"

"Just an expression. I mean, she has to be somewhere, right? I don't have a clue, believe me."

"Do you know a tall, gaunt man?" I asked, and I described the man I had seen with her in the cafeteria.

"No one like that. He doesn't sound her type."

A key turned in the door. It meant nothing to me, but it did to Ted Marshall. He got up with a grunt, clutched at his ribs. A short, dark man in army fatigues came in. The newcomer took three quick steps into the room.

"Ted, I—"

He saw me, gave a small gasp, almost rose up on his toes, and his hand flew to his mouth. A girlish gesture, startled and automatic. He looked like a girl, dirty fatigues or not. Long lashes over dark eyes, a delicate face, a slender body. Yet he was no boy. Over thirty, his face lined, his bare forearms muscled. His hands were stained, had broken nails. He tried to recover, smiled coyly, waggled his hips—girlish.

"Your mother," he said, "she leave. I think now is good time . . . well . . . So introduce me to your friend."

A woman's phrase, coy. The tone, the manner—one of the boys. Ted Marshall? I looked at Marshall. His pallor was flushed pink. He ground his teeth as he spoke.

"Dan Fortune, Frank Madero—our night super. Mr. Fortune's a detective, Frank. Private."

His voice was tight. It was there all right, a "thing" between them. Both of them vibrated like nerve ends. Ted Marshall had been quick to tell Madero that I was a *private* cop, no threat from the vice squad. Oh, hell.

"Francisco," Madero said, bowed. "I am from Cuba. I come later, Ted, of no importance. The leak of the faucet. A pleasure to know you, Mr. Fortune. I am not always the janitor. Maybe I see you sometime."

He went as fast as he had come. Here to fix a leak, okay, but he had expected to find Ted Marshall here, and alone. I let Marshall break the freeze.

"He's . . . a friend, too. Nice guy. Not like most supers," he said lamely.

"Sure," I said. "If you remember anything, call me."

In the corridor I lit a cigarette, and swore. I didn't care if Ted Marshall liked orangutans, but if he swung both ways, and wanted to hide it, the mess could be complicated. If he did swing two ways, and wanted to hide it, he wasn't going to be much help. He would stay far away from the heavy boots of the police.

6

I CALLED Sarah Wiggen from a booth on Sixth Avenue. She sounded alone, and nervous.

"No, I haven't heard anything from her, Mr. Fortune."

"No news? The police? Ricardo Vega been around?"

"Nothing," she said. "I know the police still think she just went away. Perhaps she did. She does things that way."

"When she asked you to go home? You believe that?"

A silence. "No, I don't believe that."

"Sit tight. I'll call back. Maybe she'll show."

Maybe she would show, Anne Terry. I was tired, my missing arm was aching. You'd think I'd been walking on the stump. Nuts! The lost arm didn't hurt when I was tired, it hurt when I was upset, low. It's my monkey, that missing wing, where the nerves are raw. Anne Terry was still missing. In a way, I'd been with her all day. I was getting to know her, and what I knew so far, I liked, and I didn't think she was going to show up now—not on her own.

All around me the mobs of people were on their way home from the offices, the stores, the work-services, the small factories—stepping on each other's feet like refugees fleeing. Five-thirty P.M. Some brisk and hurrying, some dragging themselves, but hurrying or dragging to what? To tomorrow. Never more than one dimension at a time: ciphers at work, TV at home. Flat men in a flat world, or who could know for sure what we are? Work and perish for the sake of a copper penny. A quote? Yes, a quote. From Isaak Babel, a writer who had died the victim of a different future, but a future just as one-dimensional.

(There we go again, the malady of the sailor at sea, the dweller in solitary cafés—reading. Worse: reading and remembering.) Isaak Babel's words, and my thoughts. "A worthy laborer who perished for the sake of a copper penny . . . Ladies and gentlemen! What did our dear Joseph get out of life? Nothing worth mentioning. How did he spend his time? Counting other people's cash. What did he perish for . . . ?"

Tired thoughts on a street corner with the hordes of people pushing around me. Missing arm thoughts. Anne Terry thoughts. Was she dead somewhere for the sake of a copper penny? Had she gotten much from her life beyond Ted Marshall and Ricardo Vega? She had wanted a lot, and where the hell was she, and was Vega part of where she was? What the hell was I doing anyway? Out to get Ricardo Vega, sure. No, not now. Trying to find a girl who might not be doing anything but enjoying herself. A girl I had come to like in half a day. No, liked her that first night in the rain; the beautiful, direct, bony face; the gentle touch in a bare cafeteria; the realistic voice:

"You better fade out, Gunner."

Direct and simple—and surrounded by parasites, scavengers? Sarah Wiggen who resented not being in her life all the way, who hated her verve, spark, and who had lost Ted Marshall? Not that Anne would have had to "take" Ted Marshall.

"I don't need losers, Gunner. Bring me the winner."

A world of nothing worth mentioning for Anne Terry who only wanted to work hard for what she knew was inside her? Integrated, full, needing no help.

"I don't guess so. Mind your own henhouse."

Who minded Ricardo Vega's henhouse?

"I really dig the guy, too, except he'll never be sure enough to relax. Too bad."

Too bad? How? For her? No, she wasn't a woman who worried about "too bad" for herself, tougher. Too bad for Vega that he wasn't man enough to be her man, so had to be something else for her? Too bad, what she had to do?

"You better fade out, Gunner."

Maybe I'd better fade out. Me, another loser for her? Probably. If I found her, what? Nothing. For my needs there had to be trouble for Ricardo Vega, and that meant there had to be trouble for Anne Terry. Another scavenger.

From the telephone booth I called Marty at her theater uptown. She was busy; maybe an hour, they said. I left a message—the back booth at Black's Tavern. I needed that friend now, and a drink. Because what did I do next?

I got the first free Irish whisky at Black's, but not the friend. Joe Harris was busy, the long bar packed with the office refugees staving off tomorrow with the perpetual present of booze. With my second good Irish, I carried a hamburger to the back booth. All right, what *did* I do next?

I'd spent the afternoon establishing that Anne Terry did look missing, and learning that she was a free bird who flew over the whole city, who moved quickly among strangers, who drank and played in the big, anonymous places where no one was going to remember her too well. My informers would do me no good with her. I couldn't track her through familiar haunts. There was her job, but I didn't think she would have let those she worked with into her private life. Anyway, the police would have checked there; they would have done all the routine. No, all I could do was go around the track again, and add Sean McBride —was he working for Ricardo Vega, or on his own?

The prospects didn't inspire me, and I was turning them over glumly, when I saw Marty come in. Her face drove all prospects from my mind. It was tight and angry, with the hunted, violent eyes I knew too well on her bad days. She had "bad day" written all over her. When she sat down in the booth, she didn't say hello. She ordered a martini, and her small body trembled. I waited until she'd had her first gulp.

"Want to talk about it?"

"No!" She drank. "Yes, all right. We did my scene today, twice. When we finished, Kurt took me aside. Kurt Reston, the director—when

Vega lets him direct. He told me how good I was. He wanted me to know how good he thought I was, what a future I had!" She drained her glass.

"The ease-out? Preparing you?"

"What the hell else? Get me another martini."

I waved to Joe. "Maybe not. It sounds like this Kurt Reston will fight for you."

"And lose! Unless he wants to be looking for a new job, too." Joe brought the martini, winked, patted Marty, and went back to his post. She drank, suddenly smiled. "Ah, what the hell. Kurt said I'm good."

"That's my girl." I took her hand. "Vega doing anything?"

"Looking muscular. Dazzling me with distant smiles."

"No new direct passes?"

"Just George Lehman's leering hints, and that new toad hanging around. You know, that Sean McBride. He's weird."

"Weird? How?"

"He seems to think that what he did to you ought to make me pant for him. He's proud of it. I'm too much for a one-arm."

"McBride's after you? For himself?"

"That's what I mean, Dan. First he comes after me for Rey Vega. He knows about you and me, too, and what I think of his beating you. Yet the next I know he's after me like a bull. He's got to be a little in-sane. Vega's his big chance, but Rey hates competition, and McBride could be out on his saddle."

"He likes risky games, maybe? For the kicks?"

"And he's violent, Dan. He went all tight when I called him Vega's boy. He said he was no one's boy."

"Vega could have a tiger in his fist," I said. I told her about McBride today, and what I'd been doing. "You did say earlier that you didn't re-ally know Anne Terry?"

"She's just in Vega's acting class with me. Don't you think the police can find her?"

"They get a hundred a day like her, Marty. They can't move fast or deep on such a small thing. Routine."

She drank. "You think Vega's mixed up with her?"

"I started with that in mind. Only now—"

"Now you want to help her? That's good, Dan."

"Maybe not good for her. Maybe she doesn't want to be found. She's a complex girl. You look at her, at how she lives, and she's a standard show-biz hustler. Hard at twenty-two; cool and calculating. Snubs her sister, sleeps around, sponges off men, has a 'good' address she can't afford, poses nude to draw attention. The main chance. Standard hustling."

Marty nodded. "From the little I know of her."

"No." I drank some Irish. "The girl I met wasn't hard; just direct, honest. Not calculating, but realistic. She didn't have to stop McBride, risk trouble, but she did. With that thin man in the cafeteria she was gentle, warm. Her apartment is warm, real; no front inside. She works like a dog for The New Player's Theater. It looks bigger than anything else in her life. A real theater company, and that's not a standard hustler. They work only for themselves, number one, onward and upward. Anne Terry has dreams of art, Marty, not silk sheets."

Marty finished her martini. "Add that she's good, too, Dan. Very good, not just a body on display. I've seen her."

"Okay," I said. "Two faces. In Vega's apartment she was like any hustler out to use Vega. On the street she said she really liked him, and I believed her. She said it was 'too bad' that she really liked him. As if she was saying she couldn't afford to be real! As if the face she shows the public is *manufactured*—a product to *sell* herself!"

I hunched forward in the booth. "A girl married at fourteen to some Carolina dirt farmer. She grows up, and somewhere she gets a dream—theater. She comes to New York, learns how a girl with nothing survives in New York. So she manufactures an Anne Terry to sell for any buck, short term; and behind that façade the other Anne Terry works hard for the real long term. Two worlds: the high-life hustler, and the dedicated actress."

"Not so rare," Marty said, "and not so split, Dan. She probably likes both worlds a little. Does it help find her?"

I sat back. "Makes it damn near impossible. What world do I look in for an answer? I don't know, but I've got a hunch the gaunt guy in the cafeteria is a key. He doesn't fit."

Marty thought about it. I waved to Joe for another drink. Marty wanted one, too. At least I'd made her forget her own troubles for now. She sipped her drink this time, thoughtful.

"He sounds like a farmer, Dan. Maybe her husband?"

"A man she married at fourteen? He didn't act like he'd come looking for her, and there's no sign of a husband around. No one even hinted at a husband. She lives alone. She—"

It slid into place. Just like that. The answer. She took her pay by the week. She turned every dollar, worked too much, but had no bank balance. No income tax forms at her place. Gone every weekend, even from Ted Marshall. Every Friday she drew cash—fifty dollars, always the same.

"She's got another place," I said. "Marty! Another place, and she supports it! Every Friday she goes somewhere with cash. She doesn't miss often. It even takes her away from The New Players'. It has to be damned important to her."

"Actresses work weekends, Dan. We have to."

"Maybe it hasn't come up. Has she had an acting job? The New Player's, okay—maybe the few times she missed were when The New Player's were performing weekends! It's important, and she pays. Always fifty dollars—rent, maybe, or food money?"

Marty was doubtful. "That important? A husband?"

"Maybe he's sick, maybe she loves him. I don't know. I do know that this time she hasn't come back, and she expected to."

I went to the telephone. Sarah Wiggen was still at home, still nervous, but she didn't sound still alone.

"Boone Terrell?" she said when I asked about the husband. "I suppose he's in Arkansas. He lives down there."

"Anne divorced him?"

"I wouldn't know. We never knew him, and she never mentions him. You don't think she's gone to him? That's crazy."

"You mean your whole family never knew him?"

There was a nasty kind of sigh. "We never even met him, and we didn't care. She ran off, my Daddy tore up her letters. She wrote three in a year, she never liked to write, she was in seventh grade when she ran off. After a year she stopped writing." There was a pause. "Anne's three years younger, Mr. Fortune. I should have married first! She left me to help Ma alone. I didn't care about her. Four years ago I found out she was up here. I came up, why not? Down home all the decent boys were married while I helped Ma. She never mentioned Boone Terrell, I didn't ask. We didn't get along here anyway."

"Ted Marshall?" I said.

Silence. "Not just him. She keeps away from me."

"Do you know what she does weekends?"

"Does? Sells herself in her night clubs."

"Yeh," I said.

"Do you have some idea? You sound—"

"I'll know more after I've been back to her apartment."

I hung up before she could ask me more. All I had was an off-beat suspicion. I told Marty to wait an hour. If I wasn't back, Joe would put her into a taxi. She understood.

7

THERE WAS nothing like police outside Anne Terry's building. The stream of homecomers had thinned to solitary stragglers as the last purple light faded. The street door was open, and I heard noise in the basement. I went up, hoping the lock on her door hadn't been fixed. It had been. I listened for a full five minutes. That can be a long time alone in a corridor. There was no sound inside. I took a breath, opened the new lock with one of my master keys.

The police had done a routine search now, but the place hadn't changed. It was still warm, comfortable, and just beginning to have that feel of emptiness deserted apartments get after a time. Or that could have been me—looking all day for a girl who wasn't anywhere. Only she had to be somewhere.

I started, again, with the closets—every pocket, the linings, the floors, the shelves. One concrete hint of a second home was all I needed. I didn't get it. The chests-of-drawers were no better. Books are often good for addresses, other names. Hers weren't: no inscriptions, no pieces of paper, no bookmark envelopes. I had hopes for the bathroom—drugstores use name-labels, and with luck she would have bought some medicine at her other place. She hadn't.

The desk was next. It took an hour, the silence of the apartment growing heavy on me with distant voices all around from other buildings. Over an hour, but when I found it I got all at once. A sales slip from Macy's. Among all her paid bills; a grain of sand if I hadn't been looking-for it. I didn't fault the police, I had seen it once myself. But now I knew what I wanted. A sales slip for a bathrobe, with her name and the Tenth Street address—and an address for the robe to be sent to: Terrell, 1977-A Steiner Street, Long Island City, Queens.

I took the subway. There was no pot of gold in this. Northbound from Eighth Street it wasn't crowded until we got to Forty-second Street, and I had a seat. By Rockefeller Center I sat dark in a valley of humanity hanging from hand-holds. They rocked with the train, adapted to it after long years. Some read. Some stared. Some muttered to themselves. Some hung with their eyes closed, asleep standing. The late ones who worked long hours, whipped.

In Queens I found the right bus. It let me out in one of those neighborhood business sections that fill the boroughs of New York. A thousand "downtowns" like Chinese boxes, the smaller inside the larger from the center of Manhattan out to Little Neck. The "New York" the world knows is only the heart of Manhattan, the rest a series of main streets a lot like Peoria.

The main street was crowded, the stores open late where profit hung by a fingernail. Twenty yards right or left any solitary figure on the dark side streets moved like a silent shadow in a forest. Semi-detached brick houses lined the streets, driveways beside them, the yards behind. At the corners, tall apartment houses made the semi-detacheds seem isolated, individual. In each house a family lived unique in its own eyes, individual. To a giant's microscope each family in each house was the same. That is the power and the weakness of people in mass civilization. Weakness that they believe themselves more individual than they are while the giant manipulates them. Power that they can be, in the last fire, individual beyond the giant.

Steiner Street was on a border: the border between middle-class needs and the spread of slum and industry. The same semi-detached houses, but fewer of them, surrounded by small factories, warehouses, garages. Not shabby themselves yet, the houses, but ringed by shabbiness. A street where the not-quite-poor held to the last pride of middle-class values. On its way down. Where the residents fought a rearguard action with brooms, hoses and geraniums.

The unit that had to be 1977 was the last pair on the block next to a tall warehouse. One driveway had been lost to the warehouse, and the whole semi-detached seemed squashed by the shadow of the warehouse. It would be the cheapest unit on the block. The side near the warehouse was lighted, the other side was dark. I didn't feel optimistic. In New York, even in a semi-detached where two families live so close, neighbors too often know nothing of each other. But there are exceptions, and I decided to ask some questions at the lighted side first.

How much of our life is automatic assumption? We see what isn't there, because we see what our minds expect: our minds a storehouse of prejudices, automatic notions, assumptions unaffected by observation. If I had not approached the house up the narrow walk I would have taken an oath, later, that the side I wanted was the dark side. I would have believed it completely, sure I had seen it, because my mind assumed that, since I was after a mystery, the side I wanted was the dark side. I would have been wrong. The lighted side was 1977-A. There was loud music inside. Very loud music, bright and bouncy.

When I rang the bell the music did not stop, but quick, light footsteps scrambled and literally ran to the door. There was a frantic fumbling at the lock, and the door swung wide open. I had to look far down at the tiny girl who stood there.

"I'm Aggy. What's your name?"

By her size she looked maybe three years old, but I guessed she was nearer to five. A tiny child with a round, freckled face, and big, eager brown eyes.

"Dan," I said. "Can you tell your Daddy I'm here?"

"Did you bring me something?"

She had seen my missing arm, and began to circle around me looking for it. She giggled, sure that the missing arm was a game—I had it hidden somewhere with something for her in it.

Another voice called, "Don't stand with the door open!"

It was a firm, authoritative voice, but not adult. Aggy vanished at a run. I closed the door as a second child appeared. She was drying her hands on an adult apron. The apron touched the floor. She was about seven, thinner than Aggy.

"Hello. Do you know how to bake biscuits?"

"No, sorry," I said. "Is your Dad at home?"

"I want to make some biscuits," she said, and gave an exaggerated sigh of annoyance—mimicking adults sighing.

The house was grim. A barren living room was meagerly furnished with secondhand relics: serviceable, nothing more. Some crude pieces had been built half-heartedly from packing boxes and orange crates. They had been left unpainted. Yet everything was draped and covered with random pieces of colored cloth that seemed to have no pattern, that added to nothing. Or did they add to beauty for a child, the random pieces of cloth? The efforts of a child playing house.

"Mommy loves biscuits," the little girl said.

The second room was even more barren. There was an old television set, a single armchair, and a battered record player on the floor. Toys were littered all across the floor: old toys, mostly broken. The record player was the source of the loud music, and the smaller child, Aggy, sat in the one chair with her thumb in her mouth, listening.

"I'd like to talk to your Dad," I said to the older child.

"He's not home yet. I'm making dinner."

In the kitchen a chipped, enamel-top table was set for three, but awkwardly, as if by someone with all thumbs. A package of crackers and a carton of milk were on the table. Soup bubbled on the stove. There was a box in front of the stove. The older child stood on the box to stir the soup.

"It's Lipton's chicken," she explained. "In little paper packages, you add water. I can't open cans. Aggy likes lettuce. I don't, ugh, so I have raw carrots. I hope Mommy wakes up soon; we're out of cookies for dessert."

"Your mother's here? Asleep?"

"We're too young to stay alone, silly. Only Mommy won't wake up. She's been sleeping awful long. She came home early, but Daddy had to go away. We played, but she got tired. She said maybe she'd sleep a long time, we had to play nice and not make a mess. I hope she wakes up soon. I'm too short."

"Where is she, honey?"

"In bed, of course. You know people sleep in bed."

The loud music stopped, and the smaller child yelled for a new record. The seven-year-old hurried away, fussy and exasperated—like Mommy. I found the bedroom.

Anne Terry lay on top of the bedspread covered awkwardly with a blanket. Her face was quiet and slack, her eyes closed, her hands on her stomach. A glass of water on the bed table had bubbles of stale air in it. A bowl of cereal and a plate of doughnuts were untouched on the bed table.

From her slack face, the odor, the stiffness of her cold legs, I guessed that she had been dead for maybe two days.

I took off the blanket. She wore a black slack suit and a white blouse. There was no blood, no marks, no wounds. A small bottle of pills on the bed table was half full. No violence, no pain on her face, only death. I went back out.

The smaller child was singing with her record. The older was back stirring her soup. There was a brightness to the seedy rooms as if the little girls, despite the older one's mothering, knew they were only children and needed light and noise.

I touched the older child. "What's your name, honey?"

"Sally Anne Terrell. Is Mommy awake now?"

"Not yet. Can you tell me how long she's been asleep?"

"A long time."

"Today is Monday. Do you know that, Sally Anne?"

"I know that!" She was insulted.

"Good. Do you know what day your mother went to sleep?"

"I don't know."

"Yesterday?"

"Oh, no. Before that."

"She came home early. When was that?"

"On Friday, silly. It's always Friday when she comes."

"She went to sleep Friday night?"

"Oh, no! She read to us on Friday. Daddy was gone. Next morning she went away. Saturday, I guess. Cartoons were on."

"She went out Saturday, and came back?"

"Daddy was away. Mommy came back and played. Only she got tired. She broke two glasses at dinner! She walked funny. She went to sleep. She won't wake up. We always watch *Lassie*. That's on Sunday, I know that. I gave Aggy her milk money today. She's only kindergarten, but it's important to get good habits. I stayed home with Mommy."

"That was good. When your mother said she might sleep for a long time, did she do anything? Tell you anything?"

"No. Oh, she took some aspirin, of course."

"Your Dad hasn't been home since Friday?"

"He was mad, I think. He went to drink. He gets pains."

"You didn't call him? At his work? Today?"

"Oh, he doesn't work except sometimes. We don't have any telephone."

"All right, Sally Anne. I'm going to find a telephone. Your mother is sick. I'm going to get some help."

"Okay. I'll feed Aggy."

I had to go to the main street to find a booth. I called the police. When I got back to the house, the little girls were playing a game with a kind of plastic bucket that shot colored balls all over the room. The object was to chase the balls and get them back to receptacles on the bucket first, each player having a different color. I got green. The three of us were still chasing balls and shouting when the police arrived.

8

A LIEUTENANT DENNIKEN was in charge. I didn't know him, Queens isn't my beat, but I saw the kind he was. A "cop" who lay awake nights hating the Supreme Court for coddling "evil." Law and order; but order before law. Injustice better than disorder.

"You talk when we ask, Fortune. Go sit down."

Yet he was human. He found a neighbor woman, not next door where it was still dark, but three houses down. He sent Sally Anne and Aggy with the neighbor before the assistant Medical Examiner arrived. She agreed to keep them until something was decided, if it wasn't too long, she had her own affairs. She knew nothing about the husband except that he was a bum.

"There's a sister," I said. "Sarah Wiggen. She doesn't seem to know about the kids. Mrs. Terrell lived a double life." I could have added that Anne Terry had really lived a triple life, but Denniken wasn't going to care about my abstractions.

"Shamski, get the sister's address from Fortune here, and give him the spiel," Denniken ordered.

The "spiel" was the recitation of my constitutional rights. Denniken couldn't even bring himself to say them.

"Okay, Mister Fortune, now tell your yarn," he said.

I told him the whole story except that I left Ricardo Vega out. He scowled when I had finished.

"Missing Persons and her Village Precinct are looking for her? You're sure?" He didn't like anyone in on his cases, especially not the Centre Street brass.

"I'm sure, Lieutenant."

"How come you followed up on your own? You didn't report the lead brought you out here?"

"A hunch, not a lead. I'll report now."

"No, mister. I'll report. You'll answer questions."

The assistant Medical Examiner came out of the bedroom wiping his hands with distaste. It suddenly brought home the fact to me: Anne Terry was dead. The beautiful body, the hard work, the dedication and the ambition, the strong self-reliance, were all gone. The good actress, the struggling girl, and the mother. I could hear her bony voice, "So long, Gunner." I had liked her. To the M.E. she was only decay, unpleasant.

"We'll have to autopsy before I can tell you, Denniken," the M.E. said. "A tough one. She had—"

"Hold it, Doc," Denniken snapped. "Fortune here doesn't need to know."

"I've got a client, Lieutenant."

"To find the girl. You found her. Take him in, Shamski."

"For what?" I said.

"Material witness. We need your statement—tomorrow."

"Like that?"

"You want to argue?" Denniken didn't smile.

I walked to the door without answering. I waited there for Detective Shamski. Denniken didn't seem to like my attitude, but that didn't bother me. Anne Terry could have died of natural causes. Most people do, even at twenty-two. There were no signs of violence, and the whole thing could be over for me. What bothered me was the little girls, the toys on the floor. Children make me feel sad, vulnerable, as I get older.

Detective Shamski walked me out to the squad car. He was silent, embarrassed. I didn't try to make him feel better. He had to get used to working with the Dennikens. We drove to the station, and he marched me inside. He huddled with the desk sergeant. Neither of them seemed happy. The sergeant nodded me to the desk. Shamski left looking relieved.

"I need your personal junk, Fortune," the sergeant half apologized. "Lieutenant says hold you. Material witness, your own protection. I guess he can justify it, and the Captain keeps his hands off the squad room if he can."

"Don't make waves, I understand. Can I make one call?"

Now he looked embarrassed. "Denniken said no lawyer yet. I got to work here."

"My girl," I said. "She expects me. You can listen."

"I guess that's okay."

He pushed a telephone at me. I was lucky, Marty was home. I told her I was stuck with Lieutenant Denniken, I didn't like it, and she better call The Preacher. When I hung up, the desk sergeant looked grateful. It's a mean world most of the time. "The Preacher" was a nickname for Captain Gazzo at Centre Street. My call was a message to Gazzo. So much for the sergeant's trust.

They put me in a cell. Gazzo would work man-to-man, nothing official. It took about three hours. Denniken himself came to the cell for me. He walked me to the street.

"Anything I can tell my client?" I asked.

"She's been told."

"You find the husband yet?"

"Stay out of my area, Fortune," Denniken said. "You had to get word over my head. Very clever. You know, you wouldn't like that yourself if you were me."

He walked back inside. He wasn't going to tell me anything. Maybe I'd made a mistake. On the dark Queens street I was too tired to worry about it.

I rode a slow subway into Manhattan, and called Marty. I didn't want to go home, and I didn't want to go to her place. I wanted a public place, with voices and lights. Marty said she'd meet me at The Jumble Shop bar. She was waiting when I got there. In her old clothes, her hair in a kerchief. She looked as if she'd been asleep, but I knew better.

"Studying," she said. "What happened, Dan?"

I told her.

"Oh, damn!" she said. "Those children were with her?"

"Since Saturday. Aged maybe seven and five. Their mother wouldn't wake up. The father gone. The older one took care of the younger. Nice kids, happy." When the drinks came, I drank. "That's what she did on her weekends; went to be with two little kids she had hidden in a house in Queens. Kids and a husband. Took fifty dollars out there every Friday."

"At least she went to them, was with them," Marty said.

"She lived one hell of a busy life. Mother, actress, and hustler. No wonder she was tired-looking. But she had them near her. They were a family. Now what do they do?"

"How did she die, Dan?"

"Don't know. There were some pills near her."

"Suicide? No, Dan. She was trying to be a mother even in her life, with her ambitions. She worked too hard."

"Who knows?" I said. "Maybe I never will know now. Let's just drink."

We drank. We talked about other things. After all, she had been a girl we hardly knew, Anne Terry, and we had our own lives like everyone else. When even I knew I'd had enough to drink, and had begun to talk again about Anne Terry and her hidden life, I took Marty home. Somehow, we both needed each other, needed something to hold to.

Marty had an early appointment, so I went home. I went to bed. All at once I wanted to curl into a ball and sleep without thinking. How many show-biz hustlers, or even dedicated actresses of twenty-two, struggling to advance an inch, take fifty dollars every week and go to be a mother to two little girls? Most of us are half dead all the time. Anne Terry had been very alive.

So I slept, but not well. The two little girls seemed to mix in my dreams with a lost arm. An arm is part of a man, and so is a child. Even lost, they can't be escaped. Faces in my dreams. All the faces, but always the faces of the little girls turned up to Anne Terry. They smiled as she told them that a great prince would help them all live in a castle where they would be busy and happy working every day. Ricardo Vega's face appeared with a laugh that echoed and echoed.

Then the unshaven face of Captain Gazzo, the sleepy gray eyes. Gazzo sat astride a chair with his arms folded on the high back, his chin on his arms, and watched me like an owl as he asked, over and over, how had Anne Terry died?

9

CAPTAIN GAZZO talking over and over:

"In my office it's nine A.M. You're not in my office, Dan. Why aren't you in my office? Telling me about it?"

In morning light the deep furrows of Gazzo's face are like the steel lines of a Durer engraving. No dream. Astride the chair, the owl watching me wake up, he looked like his own myth—the myth that says he never sleeps, year in and year out.

I reached for a cigarette. "How'd you get here?"

"You're not the only snooper with master keys. Let's talk about Anne Terry. Coffee? I plugged it in."

I nodded, he got two mugs of coffee, straddled the chair.

"Where are the kids?" I asked, drank coffee. "The husband?"

"Social Service has the kids, we're after the husband. Word says he's floating around Manhattan. The sister says she knows nothing, never did. She doesn't cry, Dan. She's your client?"

"Only legally," I said, and told him about Marty and my vendetta on Ricardo Vega. I don't hold out on Gazzo unless he's in an official stance with even me. When he has to be, he lets me know, and we understand each other. "Who gave the word on the husband?"

"Local bar flies out there. The Pyramid tavern. Boone Terrell was in on Friday. Got drunker than usual. Yelled about all women being whores. He ran out of cash and credit, said he had Bowery friends to stake him. We're looking."

"Jealous?"

"Or guilty."

I heard it in his voice. Anne Terry had not died of natural causes, and not of suicide. I sat on the edge of the bed.

"How?" I asked. "No marks on her, no blood I saw."

"Abortion," Gazzo said.

He has seen every way of death there is, every violence the half-sane imagination of man can think up. He says we're all crazy, and that he's the craziest for trying to stop us from feeding on each other's blood. Hate, greed and insanity he knows, but he's never learned to live with waste.

"A pretty good job, the M.E. says," he said. "Not perfect, some internal bleeding and heavy pain after she got home, but she was packed right, no infection. A real Doc could have done it. She should have made it from the cutting."

"She didn't make it."

"No," Gazzo said. "He used sodium pentothal for anesthetic. A heavy dose, not fatal, but she would have been woozy. She had pain at home, so she drank some whisky, and took some of those pills on her bed table. Prescription pills, but in one of those sample bottles the drug companies send to doctors. The M.E. thinks she was so woozy she took a double dose of the pills by mistake—took the dose twice because she forgot. The combination of pentothal, booze and pills could have killed her, but probably wouldn't have, except she had a respiratory condition, too. She felt bad, took the pills, lay down, and just stopped breathing. Bad luck all around."

The sun was breaking through the morning gray now. I put out my cigarette. Bad luck? That was all?

"Why you, then?" I said. "A Homicide Captain?"

"Yeh," Gazzo said. "We don't much like those pills, Dan, you know? Maybe just bad luck, but those pills worry us. The bottle says take two for pain. The M.E. says she probably took six—added one for good measure, then took the dose twice by accident. There were maybe ten left in the bottle, so no suicide. The kids say no one was there, but they played outside, and that house is wide open. No, we just don't like those pills."

"Someone might have known what they'd do to her?"

"Maybe. Now tell me about Ricardo Vega, and everything."

I told him; especially about the rainy night, and what Anne Terry had said to Vega and to me, and what she had done. I told him about Sarah Wiggen and Ted Marshall, and about Sean McBride at Anne's apartment.

"You think what she wanted to talk to Vega about in private could have been being pregnant?" Gazzo said.

"It's got the sound."

"That Marshall could be covering for her, and the Wiggen girl reported her missing fast—maybe she knew Anne was going to have an abortion, and got worried," Gazzo said.

"It plays," I said. "Ricardo Vega's child?"

Gazzo nodded. He got up and went to the telephone. I didn't hear all he said, but I heard Ricardo Vega's name. Gazzo came back.

"Get dressed, Dan."

I got dressed.

Ricardo Vega was waiting in Gazzo's office. He looked alert and muscular, and he wasn't alone. The business manager, George Lehman, stood wrinkled and sleepy. A small, sharp man carried a briefcase and fidgeted—a lawyer. Vega was sitting, neither sleepy nor fidgeting. When he saw me, he smiled.

"Well, Captain, I feel better now," Vega said, his dark eyes on me. "I begin to understand all this."

Gazzo sat behind his desk, lighted a slow cigarette. "What do you understand, Mr. Vega?"

"That Fortune there, he's got it in for me."

"Rey!" George Lehman said quickly.

The lawyer moved. "Mr. Vega has nothing to say until we know what this is all about, Captain. I protest this high—"

"Shut up," Vega snapped. "When I need you, I'll tell you. Both of you."

"Rey, as your lawyer I insist—"

"Don't insist," Vega said, the princely warning in his smooth voice again. "What am I, Mafia? I've got to be careful? The Captain's going to trap me? Hell," and he leaned toward Gazzo. "Fortune there hates my guts, Captain. He's out to get me. Any way he can. He thinks I'm after his girl, and he's worried. Maybe he should be. What's he got to offer?"

Gazzo looked at me. "What about it, Dan?"

"I hate his guts," I said mildly, "and he's chasing my girl. But he chases a lot of girls, and I didn't bring his name in first, the sister did."

"Sister?" Vega said. "What sister?"

"Sarah Wiggen," Gazzo said. "She reported Anne Terry missing, and she brought your name in, so we talked to you."

"You talked to me, and I told you," Vega said. "The girl's in my class, we had some drinks, no more. Who knows where she is?"

"You had more than some drinks, Mr. Vega," Gazzo said. "We found a cuff link and a tie in Anne Terry's apartment, both yours. Fortune here has given me what he heard in your apartment between you and Anne Terry. Sarah Wiggen knows, too."

Vega shrugged. "Okay, there was more, we had some good times. I still don't know where the hell she is."

"We do," Gazzo said. "She was found dead last night in a house in Queens."

The lawyer came alert like a bird dog on a scent. George Lehman licked his lips, made a sound. Ricardo Vega only stared at Gazzo at first. Then his handsome face seemed to age, grow less handsome and more human in a space of seconds. He took a deep breath, put his hands to his eyes, rubbed at his eyes and his whole face, as if he had just learned that there were a lot of things wrong with this world after all.

"The poor, stupid kid," he said.

"She had an abortion," Gazzo said.

Ricardo Vega nodded very slowly, up and down, like a man saying: Yes, I know how it is, what else is new? His hands rubbed at his thighs, his male loins.

"You're not surprised?" I said.

"Did you arrange it for her, Vega?" Gazzo said.

George Lehman stood scared, glanced at Vega. The lawyer could stand it no longer. A police Captain was openly, brazenly, asking his client if he had committed a crime! It was enough to send any lawyer into shock.

"You listen, Captain! My client—"

"Shut up, damn it," Vega said. "I told you."

"No, Rey," the lawyer stood his ground. "I can't keep quiet when the Captain goes so far. I won't."

"I liked the girl," Vega said. "My child, maybe."

Vega got up, paced a few steps but wasn't aware of his movement. He was thinking. I had a glimpse of the brain that had to be under his gaudy surface to have made him the artist he was. He made his decision.

"All right. I want to help. She was a hard kid, but I liked her. She had talent. I liked her a lot. Too bad."

It rang in my head, an echo: *too bad*. As if both of them had wished the rules of the game were different. Wished that they could have acted to other rules, or played another game.

Vega sat down, laced his fingers. "We had something more real than most of my things. Too real. I found myself too deep. Not marriage, she never asked, but we were becoming a pair, a twosome. You understand? Not just love, or sex if you want, but in our work. A team—with a girl kid! I found I was listening to her ideas, and advising her on her New Player's Theater plans. No! My work is mine, no partners."

"You dumped her? Like that. No regrets?" I said.

"A lot of regrets, Fortune, but I don't share my talent. I won't collaborate. I can't. I had to end it clean."

Anne Terry wasn't the only one who lived a double life. His voice, his tone, his speech pattern were all different now. Two men: the glib, virile swinger; and the serious artist. It was the artist we were hearing now. Or maybe seeing at work?

"She was pregnant?" Gazzo said.

"Not that I knew," Vega said. "She hung on, hounded me like the night Fortune was at my place. He told you what I said, but she had other ideas. She told my business manager she was pregnant, and sent him up to tell me she'd call in a few minutes to arrange to talk about it. She called, and I went to that cafeteria. She had her deal all arranged to offer me."

The lawyer was on the edge of apoplexy. "For God's sake, Rey! You're incriminating yourself like some—"

Vega hardly moved. "Charley, I told you. Okay?"

The lawyer could push professional integrity only so far. Vega was a big client. The lawyer backed off. If Vega was spinning a fantasy, he was doing an impressive job. He was building the image of a strong man who did his own thinking. Maybe too strong? He sat studying his clenched hands as if seeing that meeting in the cafeteria all over again.

"She said the baby was mine," he went on, choosing his words. "She'd have it, start a paternity suit. She told me she'd been married all along. Ted Marshall would testify that I'd known she was married; that I'd used lies, threats, my position in the theater, to blackmail *her* into adultery. She'd say she'd been afraid of what I could do to her, and had believed in all my offers to help her, so had given in when she really didn't want to. Then, afterwards, I'd refused to stand by her."

Vega seemed to think about it. "She made it sound pretty bad. Luck made the date airtight, she said—two weeks we spent at my Vermont farm just after New Year. She could prove she'd had no relations the week before, and not for a couple of weeks after. Since it really was my kid, the blood tests would show positive to every test. To top it all off, Ted Marshall had faked up a tape that sounded like me refusing to help her after she had told me she was pregnant, and I'd admitted it was mine. I sounded pretty nasty on that tape, arrogant."

He smiled a little ruefully. "She arranged that tape on me beautifully. Around the time we were beginning to bust up, about a month or so ago, we taped a couple of scenes from plays about lovers in trouble. When Marshall edited them some, and spliced them together right, she had what sounded like me refusing to help. It was a good job, even the voice levels were perfectly matched. It would be damned hard to prove it was a fake, and Anne was a good actress. I could picture her using that tape in court, tearfully telling how she'd had to trap me with a tape recorder after I refused to help her."

Vega looked grim, shook his head where he sat. "She didn't expect me to believe that she could really prove it all, she didn't think she had to. A jury might not believe her, but odds were that they would. Juries love the underdog, the weak against the big, important man. No, she didn't think I'd want a long court fight—adultery, lies, headlines, dirt, my whole past raked over. I'm no angel, so she didn't think I'd want to risk a battle in the open I could easily lose."

I said, "But could she really hurt you that way? In these days?"

"Blackmail doesn't always depend on real damage," Vega said, "but on possible damage. The victim afraid to risk damage."

"You thought there was a chance of damage?" Gazzo asked.

"She did, Captain," Vega said. "Anne wasn't bright. Tough, not bright. We live in a transition time. The young have free morals, but strong ethics. Free, but honest, and she was going to make me look dishonest, smelly, dirty. The older, middle-class people show a lot of backlash for rigid morality. My own money goes into my movies. I could be hurt at the good middle-class box office. My name is a draw. I could lose financial backing. The young admire me, I could become an ethical leper. *Could*, Captain. For a price, I'm safe. That's what she tried."

Gazzo said, "What price?"

"Twenty-five thousand, my name on a contract to direct one play, co-produce with her for one season, at New Player's. A little cash, and my name. She gets an abortion, I'm safe."

"You agreed?" Gazzo said, scowled.

Vega's face was like dark granite. "I grew up in a Havana slum, Captain. I don't scare, I don't pay blackmail. It was tried before. I didn't think she'd do it, but that didn't matter. I don't sell my name or my work, not ever!"

"You turned her down?" I said.

"Flat," Vega said. "I also took some positive action. You might as well hear it from me. Some friends of mine went to see Ted Marshall. When they left, he didn't want any part of blackmailing me, no. He was on my side. I never saw Anne again, and that was over two weeks ago."

"Then why send Sean McBride to Anne's place yesterday?" I asked. "To get what you'd left there, maybe?"

"McBride? I didn't send him. Why would I want to hide I knew her, the police had already questioned me?" He gave me his superior smile—the prince chiding a dull mortal. His story was over. It was like coming out of a quiet movie theater into the noise and chaos of the real city. His dark eyes glinted, "McBride said I sent him to Anne's apartment?"

"He didn't mention your name," Gazzo admitted. "You never knew she was married, had kids, lived in Queens, too?"

"She had children? Damn, no! I didn't know any of that." Vega leaned toward Gazzo. "Look, Captain. I knew a young girl; tough, determined, not bright. We talked plans, theater. I liked her. I'm sorry she's dead. Now do I go home, or do I let the lawyer start earning his pay?"

Gazzo nodded them out. Ricardo Vega was all smiles, like the champ leaving the ring. There was no formal statement; the story wasn't part of Anne Terry's death—if it was true.

"A good story, it sounds true," Gazzo said.

"Probably most of it is," I said.

"Yeh, most of it." The Captain swiveled. "She did a lot of living for twenty-two. If we have to dig in all of it, we're in trouble. Maybe Ted Marshall can help. I guess you'll want to go along, too?"

I wanted to go along.

10

MRS. MARSHALL answered our ring. Something had happened to her. The motherly face had grown longer, taken on rocky cliffs. Her dyed hair was tied back like a combat nurse prepared for hard action, all trivia put behind her. There was a bottomless stare to her eyes, as if she had seen what could lie on the other side of her hope. Anne Terry had happened.

"More police?" she said. "And you, Mr. Fortune?"

"Other police were here, Mrs. Marshall?" Gazzo asked.

"Late last night, yes. Ted went with them. He's still not back."

"Denniken," Gazzo said to me. "He's got the right, a known boy friend. If he'd learned anything, I'd know by now."

"What can Ted tell you?" Mrs. Marshall said, her voice level and quiet. "He knows nothing about poor Anne."

"He might not realize what he knows," Gazzo said. "You haven't heard from him since the other police took him?"

"He called from the police station. He said he was all right because he knew nothing. That was hours ago."

Gazzo turned for the door. "I'll stake a man here from the local squad."

I followed Gazzo. Mrs. Marshall spoke behind me.

"Do you think he was the father?"

I turned. "Probably not, no."

"If he was, he'd have married her. He wanted to anyway."

"She was already married, Mrs. Marshall."

"He didn't know. She could have divorced."

"I guess she could have," I agreed.

"She wasn't living with her husband, was she?"

"In her own way she was," I said. "Weekends. Maybe not really with the husband. More with her children."

"The police told Ted there were children." She had that expression women with grown children get remembering when their children were little. "Every weekend? With all her work?"

"She didn't miss often, I don't think."

"She must have been a good mother—in her own way."

Her eyes went vacant, considering the qualities of being a mother. I went out after Gazzo. As I walked out of the elevator into the bare lobby, I got a quick glimpse of a small man in army fatigues ducking behind the basement door. I found Gazzo on the street beside his car. He'd already called for a local man. A Captain of Detectives has more than one case.

"You want a lift?" he asked me.

"I'll hang around for a while."

Gazzo got into the back seat of his car. He's not one of those high-rankers who like to prove they're just-plain-cops by poses like riding up front with their drivers, scorning the soft privileges. Gazzo says he likes soft seats and thoughtful privacy as befits his rank and age.

I waited for the squad detective. This was one of my areas, and I knew him when he walked up: Detective (Second Grade) Leo Puskis. A nice cop, Puskis—too nice to make First Grade unless he gets lucky, or gets shot in the line.

"It can't be much if you're in it, Danny," he grinned.

"It isn't," I said, "but Gazzo thinks big."

"What Captain Gazzo thinks, I think. Fill me in."

Nice. Not many detectives ask a private to fill them in, it's not proper. I gave him the high points, and a better description of Ted Marshall. He went up to the Marshall apartment to wait. I went down into the basement. It was a neat basement, as meticulous and scrubbed as a Dutch housewife's kitchen. There were three apartments for superintendents. One was empty, one was locked and silent. The third had slow music behind the door, and an engraved visiting card taped to the door: Francisco Orlando de Madero y Huerta. I had to knock twice. The music didn't stop, but the door finally opened.

"Yes, mister?" It was the small super, Madero. "Hey, it's Mr.—?"

"Dan Fortune."

"Sure." His lashes fluttered. "You come to see me?"

He made a fluid motion until his weight all rested on his left leg, his left hip thrust sideways—the way a woman stands to challenge a male with her body. A posture of assessment, of provocation. It was unnerving how a small, thin, hipless male could seem so female with a few gestures, phrases.

"No, Frank. I want Ted Marshall."

"You don't want me?" He pouted.

I had no doubt he was homosexual, or bi-sexual—he wasn't effeminate; a man, not a woman. The phrases, the mannerisms, were too natural to be an act. But there was tension in his dark eyes, and he wasn't really interested in me. He was putting on an act—now, for me. His mind wasn't on my body, it was on my reason for being there.

"I want to talk to him, Frank," I said.

"I tell him when I see him. Okay?"

"There's another detective upstairs. He's going to have to talk. Why not practice on me? He might learn something."

"More policemen?" He glanced back into his apartment. A concerned gesture, protective of something inside his rooms.

"Ted better get used to it," I said.

"Yes," Madero said, serious, "I guess maybe."

His act slipped away leaving almost a new face: firm, even strong. We all live various acts, have public faces to tell other people what we are, and what we are feeling, at any given moment. We have friendly faces for friends, loving faces for our lovers, responsible faces for business. We have a real face, too, more complex because aimed at no one special, for ourselves. A homosexual doesn't think all the time of his sex, any more than a sailor thinks always of the sea. His homosexuality isn't all of him. Frank Madero's real face was like that of any other man concerned with serious demands.

"Okay, you come in, Mr. Fortune."

His living room was as austere as a monastery cell on a Greek mountaintop no one had visited since the Crusades. All the furniture had a medieval look—the dark, massive pieces you see in cathedrals, bare and hard as if there was merit in discomfort. There were religious pictures on the walls, and giant crucifixes with dead Christs bloody on them.

"He is there," Madero said. "In the bedroom."

The bedroom hit me like a blow—sensual, gaudy, with a giant bed, mirrors, purple hangings and a thick rug, all perfume like a steaming boudoir. The contrast made the living room seem like a penitent cell, an atonement for the bedroom.

"Teddy," Madero said, "Mr. Fortune wants he should talk."

Ted Marshall lay flat on the bed wrapped in the slow music from a record player. He needed a shave. His tie and jacket were off, and his shirt was open far enough to show the top of the bandage around his rib cage. The scars and bruises on his face stood out livid, and his shirt was dirty. He wasn't smoking. He wasn't doing anything. I didn't think he even heard the music.

"Leave me alone." His soft voice was thick, not pleasant now, like a man sunk in a stupor.

"Can't be done," I said. "You know it."

Marshall moved against invisible ropes. "I already told the police. How much more? Anne's dead. She's dead."

His shoulders and legs moved in an aimless motion, slowly as if movement was painful. His cool manner, the swinger with no strings between him and Anne Terry, was far gone. It looked like he had been tied to Anne Terry not with string but with thick rope. Frank Madero bent down to him.

"She is gone, Teddy," the small super said. "You must talk about it, yes?" Madero looked up at me. "Ask him what you got to, Mr. Fortune."

Ted Marshall turned his head away. Deep inside his stupor like a man under thick water. His whole body, slow movements, seeming to say: What does it matter? I'm finished.

I said, "Did you pay for the abortion, Ted?"

His head jerked around. "No! Damn you—"

"Did you send her to the abortionist?"

"No!"

"Do you know who did pay, or where she went for it?"

"No!"

"Okay," I said, "now for your lies. You said you—"

His eyes widened. "It's no lie! I don't know—"

"Vega," I broke in. "You said you knew nothing about Anne and Vega. That was a lie. You said you'd fallen off a ladder. That was a lie. Don't try to squirm out. Vega already told us about the blackmail and the beating."

He started to turn his head away again—what did any of it matter—but stopped, his empty gaze up toward the mirror on the ceiling. "Vega killed her. It was his kid, for real. After he tossed her over flat she was busted up, and mad, too. I guess she really liked the bastard. Only she was going to make him pay, get something out of it. That's when she got the blackmail idea."

"And you were part of it, the witness. You faked that tape to make him look very bad?"

"I'm pretty good with electronic stuff," Marshall said. "She was sure it would work, we'd get plenty for our theater. I guess she wasn't too smart." He seemed to be seeing Anne in the ceiling mirror. "Then last week two of them came to me at the theater. George Lehman and some blond muscleman. I was alone; they beat me pretty bad. I never could take pain. I was scared, too. I mean, if I didn't—?" He squirmed under his heavy, invisible ropes. "I gave them the tape, signed a paper saying I didn't know anything."

"So then you had to arrange an abortion for her?"

"No! I told you I don't know about that! I never saw her after Thursday!"

"You think she went through it on her own? After Vega wouldn't pay?"

He was silent, a kind of deep fear in his eyes. "I don't know. Maybe Vega did pay—something. After they beat on me, she was madder than ever. She said she'd still get him. Maybe she went on with the blackmail on her own. Maybe he paid, and arranged the abortion. Maybe he fixed the abortion so she'd die! He wanted her dead!"

Frank Madero sat in the corner, looked at the floor. Ted Marshall stared up at his own unshaven face in the ceiling mirror. Ricardo Vega a murderer?

"Can you back that up at all, Ted?" I asked.

"The way she looked, what she said. She was tough."

"When you saw her on Friday?"

"I didn't see her Friday! I told you! I went like always, and she wasn't home. I never saw her!"

"Did you know she was planning to go home to North Carolina? Maybe to recover after an abortion?"

"No. Why would she? She had her family in Queens."

"You knew she really went to Queens on weekends? You knew she had a husband and children?"

"No! I swear I didn't know!" He came up on one elbow, his thick voice taking on urgency. Fervent that I know he didn't know. Guilt for making love to a married woman with children? A modern free swinger like Marshall? "Anne never told me about any of that!"

"Ted did not know," Frank Madero said. "She keep it all very secret. She don't tell."

"You knew Anne, Madero?" I asked.

"I have that honor, yes. A nice woman."

I looked down at Marshall. "Just what did she say?"

His eyes closed up, flicked away. "If I was chicken, she wasn't. Maybe I was scared green; she wasn't. You got to take risks. Life wasn't worth living without risk. You have to live your own way. Hold back and you're dead. Like that."

It was Marshall's thick voice, but the words belonged to Anne Terry all right. I could hear her, "You got to take risks, Gunner. Hold back and you're dead." The question was: had she acted on her words, gone on with the blackmail of Vega?

"You have any real proof, Marshall?"

"No."

"Are you going to tell the police about it? "

"Why not? I've got nothing to hide."

I looked at Frank Madero. "Nothing to hide?"

Madero's eyes were flat. "We are not lovers, if you mean that. We are friends. It is possible, you see?"

"Then get your 'friend' up to his apartment. Don't make the police find him. You don't have to mention me."

Madero nodded; he understood. Gazzo wouldn't be happy about me going off on my own to Marshall. I guess I just wanted to nail Ricardo Vega myself, if I could. Ted Marshall said no more. He seemed almost paralyzed on the bed.

I went up to the street, and called Marty from a Sixth Avenue booth, but there was no answer. At her theater they said she wasn't on call until later. I wanted to talk to her over lunch, so decided to give her an hour.

Anne Terry's apartment was near. Maybe I could find some evidence to show that she had gone on with her blackmail.

11

A FAT WOMAN in a housedress with a cigarette hanging from her mouth was sweeping out the vestibule of Anne Terry's building. She gave me a smile, hummed at her work. The smile faded when I showed an old badge and said I wanted Anne Terry's apartment. It wasn't me who faded the smile, it was the dead girl.

"Awful. She was a fine girl. Straight and on the line. Maybe she liked men too much. Women are all born lonely and too eager. That's nature's way, I guess."

"I guess," I said. "Did you know her men?"

"Some, not many. She didn't broadcast."

"A Ricardo Vega? You saw him Friday or Saturday?"

"Nope. The cops asked me that. He's that big shot, right? What was she doing with a man like him?"

"A little blackmail, maybe," I said, watched her.

"Anne? I'd have to know more to know about that. Ain't no one you know for sure what they are, but I got to hear reasons, and know who says what. All I know, she was nice."

"She was nice," I said. "Can I have the key?"

"Don't need it. A friend's up there now."

I went up carefully. The "friend" could be Sean McBride again, or Ricardo Vega, or anyone. The door was open. I found him bending over the old desk, and recognized the hunting-lodge clothes: Emory Foster, the florid friend of Sarah Wiggen. An open suitcase was on the floor, filled mostly with photo albums and books. The heavy man heard me and turned.

"Mr. Fortune. You're still at work?"

"I'd like to know more about what happened," I said.

"So should I," Emory Foster said. "Poor Sarah is taking it quite hard. She asked me to get some things of hers Anne had."

"I didn't think she cared much about Anne."

"They were sisters, Fortune."

"Not close," I said. "You said you never knew Anne?"

"No, I didn't."

"You're an old friend of Sarah's, though?"

"A friend, not so old. She doesn't have many friends."

"How'd you meet her?"

"She's interested in writing. I teach a class."

"You're a writer, Mr. Foster?"

He gave a small shrug. For a thick, florid man he was subdued, tentative. He looked like a man who should roar and slap backs, hold forth at some artistic party full of celebrities, be photographed kneeling beside a lion he had shot. That kind of man, but who had been cut open and hollowed out. A shell, isolated inside a floating bubble.

"I write," he said. "Free-lance, teach a few classes. I do advertising copy, some stories. Small beer."

"For the theater?"

"No, not for the theater."

"Is it much of a living?"

"I survive, Mr. Fortune. A serious writer who doesn't find a clique of elite, or command an obvious market, hasn't much chance. So I write my books which no one will publish, and make a living doing copy, teaching, and writing trash under pseudonyms." He shrugged, stepped away from the old desk. "That seems to be all that Sarah asked me to get. Can I help you with anything? You're looking for who helped her?"

"If anyone did."

"I suppose she could have handled it alone. A tough girl, they tell me. You'd think she would have found a real doctor."

"Maybe she did. Maybe the curette slipped." I was really wondering if someone could have known what the combination of drugs would do to her?

"A real doctor would have cost a lot of money," he said. "Not to mention influence to force the risk. I wonder who she knew with both money and influence?"

"I wonder," I said

"Yes," he said. "Well, I'll leave that in your hands. I better get back to Sarah. I have my own work to do."

He went, and I searched again. The desk was a mess by now. I found no whisper of blackmail. The file was no better. It, too, had been manhandled, everything out of order. The place had been over-searched, like a field with too many footprints. I called Marty before I left. She still didn't answer.

I took the subway to Seventy-second Street, walked up beside the spring park. Even on a weekday it was crowded. There were the old with nothing to do, their years of service rewarded with idleness and the slow starvation we proudly call social security. (We're a narrow Puritan nation at the core. We grudgingly keep our old alive, but make sure they have no joy in it.) The odd and unemployable fed pigeons, and stared wondering into space. In a field, young men played soccer while their women encouraged in some foreign tongue. Without work, they played the sport of their homeland to know they still existed. We're a rich nation, we can afford to waste lives.

We can also afford to let a woman take time off when her sister dies. Sarah Wiggen was at home. She stood with her arms hugging herself as if cold. She wore black. It didn't help her to look like her sister. Yet I could see, again, that she was really a pretty woman—her drabness was inside, behind the lusterless eyes.

"What do you want, Mr. Fortune? It's over."

"You're sure, Sarah?"

She was shivering. Her eyes saw far away or long ago. Maybe both—North Carolina and a young sister she had hated for marrying first and leaving her to hold the bag on a dirt farm. She saw something much closer in time and space, too. Herself, maybe, and her hate.

"How much did you really know, Sarah?" I asked.

"Know?"

"I wondered about how fast you ran to the police. You knew about Queens, her kids, the abortion."

"No!" She hugged herself. I waited. She sat down on one of her sterile chairs. "I knew she was pregnant. I guessed what she planned to do when she talked about going down home."

"So you knew where she was? You knew she was dead?"

"Dead?" Some small life flashed in her slack eyes. "You don't think I'd have left those children alone with her? No, I didn't know about Queens, or any children. I didn't know where she was." Her hands moved to her belly. "Are they . . . nice children?"

"You haven't seen them?"

"I didn't want to, yet. Are they pretty, like Anne?"

"I think so. She never told you she had children?"

"I guess she didn't think the family deserved to know. Up here I suppose she wanted to keep them apart from her . . . her life here. I knew about Boone, yes, but I really thought he was in Arkansas. Have they found him?"

"Not yet. They have the kids in a shelter. Maybe you should go to them. They need someone."

"Yes," she said. "What will happen to them and Boone?"

"That depends on Boone and the state," I said. "Okay, you suspected abortion. Why report her missing? The noble sister trying to stop her?"

Her chin came up, and I saw a little of Anne's boniness in her face. "No, not noble. Jealous. Plain female fury. I wanted to make trouble—for both of them."

"Anne and Ricardo Vega?"

"Ted Marshall. I was sure Ted was the man."

"He dumped you for her?"

"I thought we had . . . something. I met him in acting class when I first came here. I burned to be an actress, and I liked Ted. I suppose I still do. Then Anne met him. He never called me again. Not once! I quit everything, took a safe job."

Her lusterless eyes looked like mud. I was getting the first real clue to the drabness inside Sarah Wiggen. A body full of dead dreams. Anne's dreams had been alive, vivid.

"What did you expect the police to do, Sarah?"

"Catch them, prove the abortion, send Ted to jail. I don't know. When she didn't call Sunday evening, I was half scared for her, and half hoping she was sick and Ted would be caught."

"All right," I said. "What about Ricardo Vega?"

"I don't care about him."

"The baby was his, almost sure. Anne didn't say anything about Vega, a deal, maybe a payoff?"

"No, but she wouldn't have told me about Mr. Vega."

"Think! That last call, when she talked of going home. She said nothing about plans, hopes, her future?"

"She just said she was tired, wanted to go home to rest. She did say she'd have a surprise for me, would pay my fare. She seemed anxious to have me go. But I—"

"A surprise? Money? Nothing more?"

"I wasn't going. I didn't think about it."

"Anyone been here? Vega? Friends of his?"

"Only Mr. Foster. He offered to go to Anne's and get some things I wanted. When you rang I thought it was him."

"He hasn't been back yet?"

"No, he—" The downstairs buzzer rang. "There he is."

She went to release the street door, and waited at her door as footsteps came up slowly, limping. Footsteps are distinctive, conjure up a mental picture of the man, and the steps coming up didn't make me see Emory Foster. I went for the door.

Sarah Wiggen was staring out.

I pushed her aside. He stood at the top of the stairs. Tall, stooped, his work clothes crusted with gutter grime, his pale eyes watery and red with booze and, maybe, grief. The gaunt man from the cafeteria. He tried to run, but he was shaky, weak. I got my hand on his arm, enough to ruin his balance, and he slipped, fell, crashed down the stairs to the next landing. I jumped down after him. Groggy, he tried to get up. I kicked him in the stomach. He fell back, gasping, and stared up at me. I put my hand into my pocket, held a foot aimed at his chin.

"Call Captain Gazzo, Sarah." I gave her the number of Gazzo's private office. "Tell him I found Boone Terrell."

12

GRAFFITI COVERED the walls of the Interrogation Room. A generation of janitors had tried to scrub them off. They had given up, and settled, puritanically, for scratching over the obscene ones. It left plenty of reading: *Johnny Knucks, I'll never learn . . . Little Sal been here and gone . . . You'll be back, Sal . . . Rory Connors, a bum rap . . . I'm sorry, Marge, I'm sorry. . . .*

Gazzo said, "Tell us where you've been, Terrell."

Boone Terrell sat in the chair under the light. Gazzo half-sat on the bare table. Three other detectives in shirt sleeves, guns prominent for intimidation, stood spaced around at the edge of the circle of light. I leaned on a wall, read graffiti, and listened to Gazzo work.

"Drunk, Captain," Terrell said. "I drink some."

Terrell's voice had the shakiness of a bad hangover, very bad. Under the hangover it was a firm voice, with a strong regional twang of the South, but without any whine. The voice of a decent farmer. His big hands shook, but that was booze, too. He sat like a man who didn't scare easily, a slow rock against threats or danger. The hands stuck out of his sleeves again, as if he never could find clothes that fit. His face was paler than ever, but not flabby, and his sunken eyes seemed more stunned than worried. He continually brushed at the caked grime on his clothes as if ashamed to be seen so dirty.

"I guess you do," Gazzo said. "A routine binge?"

"The weekend, Captain. You know how that is."

"Don't we all? Why'd you go to Sarah Wiggen?"

"You know, family an' all. I ran out of money."

"Did you know we were looking for you?"

"Hell, no, Captain. I sure didn't."

"Don't you want to know why we were looking?"

Terrell brushed dirt. "I guess I know."

"You guess you know," Gazzo said. "Then why didn't you come in? No, never mind for now. We checked you out, Mr. Terrell. You drink, sure, but you don't binge. Your local Queens pals say Boone Terrell he drinks, but he never goes on a binge. No sir! Boone Terrell has two kids, he takes care of his kids. Oh, sometimes he'll tie one on over a Friday or Saturday night, but never any longer. His wife comes out from somewhere on the weekends, so sometimes he gets drunk, but not often. No, Boone Terrell he watches his kids, stays with his wife."

Preacher Gazzo, Captain Mouth. They say, the thousands who have faced his verbal barrage, that when he starts talking, lawyers plead guilty. Boone Terrell only looked at him.

"I guess it's true? My Annie's dead?"

Gazzo walked away into a corner. Terrell's eyes followed him. That's one of the tricks, the walkaway. Prisoners, or witnesses, want to please their interrogator. Deep down, somehow, they all want to please, as if that will make them safe. Sergeant Jonas took Gazzo's place. Jonas is the hard questioner.

"You're saying you're not sure she's dead?"

"I guess I just don't want to be sure," Terrell said.

"Then how did you know? You sneaked out there Saturday, right? Sure; your wife, another man's kid in her. You helped her out, gave her some extra pills, killed her!"

"Annie died from pills? I never did hold with pills," Terrell said. "Saturday? The kids was all alone—with her?"

I said from my wall, "Sally Anne took good care."

Terrell nodded. "Sally Anne's a good kid." He wiped at his face with his big hand. "Word got around to me. From that Queens saloon. Fellows told fellows to tell me."

"When did word get to you?" Jonas asked.

"About morning."

"You mean today? Why did you stay away Sunday, even Monday? Your wife always went back to Manhattan on Sunday night. You stayed away, left your kids alone? Why? Because you knew she was dead, you were afraid to go back even for your kids?"

"You got it wrong," Terrell said. Hangover or not, he had an odd dignity. "Annie, she come early Friday. Said she was goin' down to Carolina with the kids, but not with me. We had us a fight. I walked out. I didn't go back 'cause I figured she was gone. I never knew about that abortion. Didn't know she was that way. I guess it wasn't mine."

Sergeant Jonas glanced at Gazzo. The Captain drank a glass of water, walked back to sit on the table in the light.

Gazzo said, "You married her when she was fourteen. You must be twenty years older than she was. Tell me about your life with her, Terrell. How did you get to New York?"

Terrell nodded. "I was thirty-five when we met up, been married once before down Arkansas. I was up Carolina visitin'. We had us a dance, Annie was there. She'd sneaked out on her folks. She was real beautiful. She liked me, and I told her I had my own place. A woman down that way likes her own place, so marryin' with older fellers ain't so special. We married up, and I took her back to Arkansas. Her people cut her off, and that kind of hurt her. I guess my place wasn't like she'd figured, neither. When we had Sally Anne and Aggy she didn't even write her Ma. I guess she was ashamed, the life I give her. A hard-rock farm, no better than her Daddy had."

"How did she get the idea of New York and the theater?" Gazzo asked. "A fourteen-year-old from a Carolina farm?"

"We got TV, Captain, and there was this summer acting place over to Huntsville. I give her a bad life. I never got to no school. All I know is hand farming. She had two kids and not even a cash crop for maybe a decent dress. It wasn't goin' to get better. Government people come down and spend more money than God got sinners improvin' farming. All that does for niggers and folks like me is send us walking. We ain't needed."

"So you walked up here?" Gazzo said.

"She done. Eighteen. I did what I could down home. The kids missed Annie; me, too. She missed the kids, maybe me, too. She wrote, said come on up we'd figure out something. I was losin' the farm anyway, not that there was much worth losin'. She got us the place in Queens. I tried to work. The Government don't do so much for us when we comes up here after we got no place down home. I got a bad leg, it pains me. I ain't smart, got no work for up here. Odd jobs. Had one once for six months 'fore I got laid off. Annie brought money every week. I lied, got welfare. She come out weekends."

Gazzo said, "You took it; the way she lived alone, how she made her money?"

"You ever see her, Captain? Alive, I mean? Know her?"

I said, "I did, Boone."

"Then you know why I hung around. What was I about to do in Arkansas alone with the kids and no better off? Up here anyways I seen her regular. There was some money."

"You met her in the city, too?" I asked. "Regularly?"

"Not much, she got to keep us hid. If I was in town, she'd see me a few minutes if she could."

"Who watched the kids if you were in town, or boozing?" Gazzo asked.

"Baby-sitters if I had money. Most times Sally Anne took care. What else we supposed to do? Everyone got a right to some livin' of their own. Her Ma taught Sally Anne good. Annie was a good Ma. Tried real hard for the kids, even for me."

"And for herself," Gazzo said. "The big ambition."

"Ain't a person entitled to what she wants, too? Try for it, least-ways?" Terrell said. "I ain't got much schoolin', but it seems to me we all got our wants, and who says a woman got to forget it all 'cause of what she done at fourteen? She done her best for her kids, and worked for herself, too. Worked like a field hand. She had to keep us hid, she had to get men to help her out. Sure, it made me feel bad. Sometimes she even had to come in on a date Saturday night, but what else did Annie have to help her? She could've done better without us, left us in Arkansas. She didn't. She was good to us."

We were all silent for a time. Terrell sat with his big hands clasped between his knees, his head down. The detectives just stood. I read some more graffiti: *I'm sorry, Marge, I'm sorry . . . George M. took a plea . . . So long, Georgie. . . .*

Gazzo said, "An interesting story, Terrell. You thought a lot of Annie. You expect us to swallow that you went on a big binge just because she was taking the kids to North Carolina? It won't play, Terrell, not with that story."

For a time Terrell sat motionless, head down. Then he took a deep breath. He raised his head. For an instant, a flash, I had a peculiar feeling that he had expected the Captain to react in exactly that way. He began to nod.

"I guess you figure me too good," he said. "She told me she was carrying. She told me what she was fixin' to do. It wasn't mine, only maybe it was, too, see? Who wouldn't go get drunk? By Saturday I got worried, though, so went and watched her come home. She looked okay to me, so I come into town an' took me a good drunk. I was dryin' out this mornin' when some fellers got word to me. I snuck on out to Queens. I saw cops, and the kids was gone, so I knew it was true. I come back in the city to drink some more. I was broke, so I went to Sarah."

I said, "Did you know she tried to blackmail Ricardo Vega?"

"She talked some," Terrell admitted. "She said maybe we'd have some money; us and for her theater. Said it was good I was sick the week before she took them two weeks away in January, and she was alone in Queens. Said it was good I got one kind of blood type. I figured she was fixin' to squeeze this Vega, only I never did know what happened about it. The Vega feller fixed it up for her to get rid of the kid. She had somethin' wrote down in case Vega couldn't take her to the place on Saturday. I guess this Vega knew the Doc who done it."

For a moment, coming like that in his slow voice, the words seemed unimportant enough. A slow bombshell, delayed. But the words were heard after a few beats, and Gazzo stood up in a kind of slow motion.

Gazzo said, "She told you Ricardo Vega arranged the abortion? That he was taking her to the doctor himself? Going with her?"

"Yes, sir, she said that. Vega's a name you remembers."

"What about Ted Marshall?" I asked.

"Never heard about him. I guess I didn't want to know about all her fellers. Just her, and me, and the kids. That's what I wanted. Don't just figure what I do now. I got no money, no work. How do I keep the kids? Could take 'em down Arkansas, or send them to her folks in Carolina. Annie wouldn't like none of that for the kids." He sighed deeply, as if hearing Anne Terry and her plans for her children. "Well, you think I can see the kids anyway, Captain?"

"I'll fix it," Gazzo said. "We've got no reason to hold you now. But we're going to check your story and your movements all the way. You understand?"

"You got your job. I thank you kindly for the kids."

Terrell stood up, and Gazzo instructed Sergeant Jonas to arrange for Terrell to go to his children. Gazzo nodded to me to follow him out. He didn't say anything until we were both seated in his shade-drawn office, and he had a cigarette.

"Well, Dan?"

"What does Terrell gain by lying?" I said. "Revenge?"

"He's got stone in him, Dan," Gazzo said. "A man like that can do a lot if he thinks he has to. But just for revenge on one of her men? Anyway, all we have is his word for what she said. His word against Vega's. We'll need more."

"You'd think he could make a better lie if he was after Vega," I said.

"Yeh, you would," Gazzo agreed. He stood up. "Let's go and talk to Vega."

13

RICARDO VEGA didn't like our reappearance. He met us at his door in a sweat suit under a cashmere topcoat. He wore Wellington boots, and looked ready to go out. The boots and slim sweat suit made him look like some dashing cavalier. An overaged cavalier, his face tired.

"I'm due at rehearsal, Captain. I've got too many problems in my show to waste time."

"We won't take long, Mr. Vega," Gazzo said. He didn't exactly push inside, or menace Vega, but we went in.

"I'm sick of that one-armed pariah," Vega said, as much to assert himself against Gazzo as anything else. "Get him out."

"Mr. Fortune is licensed to help us. He's helping," Gazzo said. "We'll wait if you want your lawyer."

"I want," Vega said, "and I have work to do."

He vanished into an inner room. Gazzo sat in his coat on an ornate Empire chair. Somewhere in the vast apartment Vega began to shout. He had been outfaced, he had to fight back against those he could dominate. George Lehman, the business manager, appeared at the inner door. Gazzo watched him without expression. Lehman went away, and the distant shouting began again.

In the late sunlight the mammoth living room had a dusty look. With its fussy, overcrowded furniture, and walls of paintings, it was somehow closed in and untouched by open space. A room that lived only at night. A room for the people who moved through it. They are night people, those who live on the high echelons of the successful business of art. They exist indoors in rooms like this. A narrow life of written words, canvas colors, shaped stone, and the judgment of each other. Always indoors and night, even when they were out in the daylight. They carry their world with them, hear the same analytical voices, in New York or Paris, Tokyo or Montego Bay.

Gazzo came alert an instant before Ricardo Vega returned to disturb my reverie. It was obvious that the apartment had a rear entrance—the lawyer was with Vega.

"Okay, let's get on with it," Vega said, impatient.

He still wore his sweat suit. Slim, but older in daylight.

"Let me, Rey, will you?" the lawyer said. "Is it the same matter, Captain? "

"Same thing," Gazzo said, and stood.

"Is there a warrant involved now?"

"Just some talk for now."

"I don't like that, but what's on your mind?"

Gazzo told them. What Boone Terrell had said, word for word, and nothing more. No judgments, no guesses. The lawyer bridled. Ricardo Vega shrugged.

"I never heard of Boone Terrell," Vega said. "He's lying."

"He didn't say he knew you," Gazzo said. "Just told us what his wife told him. Her you did know."

"She never said that, how could she?" Vega said. "If she did, she was raving or out to get me. Cause me trouble."

"She didn't know she was going to die, Vega," Gazzo said.

I said, "Why would Terrell lie? Any ideas?"

"No," Vega snapped, "and you keep out of it. You I don't have to put up with. Captain, I don't love authorities, but I want to co-operate. Only this is ridiculous. The man's lying."

The lawyer said, "Mr. Vega doesn't intend to be pushed around, Captain. We don't threaten, but he has position, power, and standing. He's an important man. Unless you have more to—"

Vega said dryly, "They know who I am, Charley."

"Let's say she was lying," Gazzo said, unaffected. "Why?"

"Who could know, Captain?" Vega said. "For her husband, perhaps. Maybe she liked to drop my name, I get that all the time. A name to satisfy the husband. Maybe to get him to come after me for revenge?"

"Did he?" Gazzo asked.

"If he did, I never noticed."

Gazzo said, "I don't figure him for revenge."

"I hope not. I'm too busy for any games."

The lawyer said, "You appear to be working very hard on a small crime, Captain. A simple abortion."

"I want the abortionist, and maybe someone set it up, even took part," Gazzo said. "Then there's the pills. She didn't exactly die of the abortion. She took wrong pills in combination with sodium pentothal. Maybe someone knew they would kill her, knew that for her the combination was extra lethal."

The lawyer was unable to believe his ears. "Murder? You suggest murder? No more, Rey! Get a warrant, Captain."

"No, wait," Vega said, waved, "Murder, Captain?"

"It's a possibility," Gazzo said.

"Rey!" the lawyer cried.

"Why, Captain?" Vega said. "I mean, think! An abortion alone ends any threat to me, right?" He leaned toward Gazzo, ticked off his points on his fingers. "Say I even paid her off. After the abortion no more threat, so why kill her?"

"To get the payoff back," Gazzo said. "That forced contract, especially. Your work and name means a lot to you, right?"

"A few bucks, and one bad contract? Please, Captain."

"I did some checking," Gazzo said. "You haven't had a money success in years. You get paid good for acting, but your own company is shaky. I figure that's what's important to you—where you do it all: write, direct, act and spend your own money. The whole deal, and the critics haven't been so nice to your shows, either. You've been losing some money, getting lumps from critics, and word says you're having a harder time getting backers. That could make a man more touchy about bad publicity. You admitted she maybe could have hurt you. Maybe she had more against you than you let on. You might have been more scared than you look. This show you're doing now, it's a big stake, right? You've got a lot riding on it."

Gazzo was a good cop, I've said it before. He works carefully and deep, looks under all the rocks. Ricardo Vega seemed to grow older before my eyes as Gazzo talked about him, and I felt a crawling sensation on my neck. Vega *was* worried, unsure. Sometimes great artists are on the way down when they look like they're on top. There's always a reputation lag. When I thought about it, Ricardo Vega's big triumphs were years old now.

"I'll bet people underestimate you, Captain," Vega said.

"Not so much anymore," Gazzo said mildly.

"Maybe not," Vega agreed, his dark eyes steady. "You do your work well. All right, I've told you I didn't kill anyone, and know nothing about Anne Terry. That's all I can do."

Gazzo nodded. "I guess so. Well, we'll go work on it some more. Thanks for the time."

I said, "You know a man named Emory Foster, Vega?"

"No," he snapped, then his eyes flickered to me. "Emory Foster?"

"Yeh," I said. "Heavy man, red-faced, maybe fifty or maybe younger. A free-lance writer of sorts. A friend of Anne Terry's sister Sarah Wiggen."

"No," he said. He was looking at me, but I had a feeling he didn't see me. "I don't know him."

He turned, and then seemed to look at his walls of paintings in the fading sunlight. Maybe Gazzo talking about his troubles had gotten to him. I heard Anne Terry's bony voice, "He'll never be sure enough to relax, Gunner." He looked at his paintings as if he saw them all melting away, the colors dripping.

"Next time, Captain," the lawyer said, "bring a paper."

Vega came from his trance. "Come when you want, Captain. I've got nothing to hide. Now, damn it, I've got work to do. Where the hell's my coat?"

He strode out of the room calling for George Lehman. The lawyer chewed on his lip. Gazzo led me out, and rumbled low in his throat all the way down in the elevator. He was talking to himself, and I knew better than to interrupt. If he wanted to talk to me, he would. We were being driven downtown when he did.

"Vega's got the ego to think he can get away with anything he has to. Terrell needs a reason to lie. Maybe revenge, only I figure Terrell more for direct action. There's something missing, Dan. I better go talk to Denniken."

I wasn't invited to talk to Lieutenant Denniken, which was just as well. I was starved. I hadn't gotten to lunch after all. Gazzo let me out in Sheridan Square, and I called Marty again. She still wasn't home—or wasn't answering. If I hadn't just left Ricardo Vega, I might have wondered. Instead, I was a little worried. I called the theater. She wasn't there either. They said she hadn't been on call, she might have been there at some time, and she was on call for tonight.

I wasn't really worried, Marty was a big girl, but I decided to have an early dinner at The Sevilla Restaurant. I like the *paella* at The Sevilla, and an oily-looking but bone-dry Spanish white wine they have, and the place is half a block from Marty's pad. From the bar you can see her front door.

I kicked off my badly needed dinner with an Irish and soda at the bar. I didn't see Marty, but before I was through that first drink I saw another familiar face. I told Mano behind the bar that I'd be right back.

Twilight was a clear, cool, dying pink over the spring city, and he was standing on the corner not looking at anyone. Just standing. He wore the same chino levis and black boots, but his shirt was black and Cossack now, and his jacket was faded denim. He was talking to himself—literally. His lips moved in his lean, boyish face.

"Waiting for someone, McBride?" I said.

He looked at me. "Yeh."

Just "Yeh," and looked away. I didn't seem to worry him. He stood lithe and easy, relaxed on the street corner as if his body was resting, his brain in repose. I wondered if he'd forgotten our rainy alley, but it wasn't that. I just didn't scare him. He wasn't a man who worried about the possible. He looked vaguely bored.

"It's a cute name, *Sean*. Vega going to adopt you?" I said.

"You got to have the right name."

"You here for Vega?"

He didn't answer.

"You wouldn't be looking for a contract and some money? What Vega gave to Anne Terry?"

He snickered. "That ain't what he gave her."

"Watching someone? Me, maybe?"

He moved his head in circles as if his neck hurt. After the first moment he hadn't looked at me again. He looked right, left, up, down; talked to me, but looked everywhere else. Marlon Brando. Yet not an act. McBride was himself, and Brando, at the same time. I was seeing life reborn through art. Brando, to communicate the essence of a type of uneducated, inarticulate American male, created his brilliant projection of their explosive, caged anguish through a series of external mannerisms. Those same males, instinctively recognizing themselves in Brando's masterpiece, adopted the mannerisms. Brando had portrayed the McBrides of America, and now McBride played Brando.

"You like being an errand boy?" I said. "A pimp?"

"Go away, man."

"You're rough in a dark alley from behind."

He looked at me from under his brows—Brando again. His eyes were violent yet uncertain; that caged pacing inside again. Sure of his needs, but not sure of himself in having those needs. I realized that McBride could never really think straight enough to act in his own best interest for very long. A man who would see only the moment and the need, like a lion who sees meat.

"Man, I got two arms, forty pounds, and maybe fifteen years on you. Go on away."

"Tell me what a famous movie star you'll be," I said.

"Man, you talk for a cripple."

He was right. I was no match for him, yet I had to be the brave bull, the loud rooster. Someday the mindless roosters, all hormones and square jaws, will destroy the world. There's no merit to challenging a stronger man on his terms, with his weapons. Losing with pride isn't something to build your life on. Dying bravely in battle may be noble, but it's not what you build a world on. No, I don't feel good when I talk big. I know it's only my missing arm that makes me do it.

"There's more than one kind of cripple," I said.

He went through his look-everywhere-except-at-me act. As if he didn't know what he would do with me. I had the sudden realization that he didn't know. Behind his uncertain eyes his brain was too busy—filled with dreams, hopes, and notions that remained random, uncontrolled. He literally didn't know what he wanted to do with me: fight, ignore, sneer or talk. Then he decided.

He walked away. Without another word or glance. Neither afraid of me, nor hating me anymore. He had decided to walk away, and I no longer concerned him. The instant his back was turned to me, I ceased to exist for him.

I watched him until he turned the next corner. I wasn't sure I envied Ricardo Vega his services.

14

I ATE my *paella* at the window table in The Sevilla. Marty hadn't shown by the time the coffee came. I hate Spanish desserts, so I settled for Irish in the coffee. Cognac is better, but I can afford only so much indulgent spending. I didn't see where I was going to make money in this affair.

It wasn't money I was after. Face it, I was after only one reward— Ricardo Vega skewered. I faced it. Sure, I had gotten to like Anne Terry, her hard days had deserved better than a cheap funeral. If her work hadn't been what a solemn D.D., or even an upright card shark, would have approved, we don't often choose what we work at. The options open can be pretty narrow. Sure, I burned for the kids who didn't even have a weekend mother now, but collaring someone for her death wasn't going to help them.

There are moments when a man has to look at himself. Alone is best. I was a hound on a scent. I wanted Ricardo Vega to be guilty. If I had wanted him innocent, what would I be thinking? That Vega had no motive big enough I could see.

Without Ricardo Vega, what was there?

A common abortion. A girl who had enough complications in her life, who wasn't too bright, and who was tough enough to take a hard risk. Accidental death.

A common abortion, but arranged by Ted Marshall. He seemed to be number one stud in her life at the moment. If Marshall confessed he was the arranger, the police would believe him instantly—standard and logical, no matter what anyone said about Ricardo Vega. Murder?

I didn't think Marshall was the type, but there are dark places in ambitious young men.

Boone Terrell? His own story said he was a man who would do just about anything for Anne, who accepted anything she did if she let him stay around. His story was also the kind of dog-like love that could turn fast to hate. A small straw; the straw of another man's baby? Love turned to hate, a rage in heaven that could become murder in a breath. His story an attempt to protect himself, get revenge on Vega, or both? Terrell was too quiet, too alert, too calm.

Or was there an unknown motive for Ricardo Vega, big enough? There were too many small hints. They kept coming up. Boone Terrell couldn't have arranged them all. Hints that the payoff might have been made after all: from Sarah Wiggen, Ted Marshall, Terrell himself again. Emory Foster wondering who had the money and influence for a good abortion. Terrell with his story, and Marshall indicating maybe Vega arranged it all. Sean McBride skulking around. All coincidence? I didn't think so, and where there was smoke, something had to be burning.

Gazzo said it—something was missing.

Then, too, did we limit it to men? Sarah Wiggen had known Anne was pregnant, and had more than a few reasons to hate her. Some sisterly pills? Or Mrs. Marshall with her boy to mother? That's the trouble with murder, the motive doesn't have to be rational, concrete. An urge will do, a momentary need rational only to the killer. And murder itself was only a thin possibility; simple chance bad luck more probable.

Like a scientist, you make an assumption and go on from there. An assumption from the facts you have. I had made an assumption at the start—Ricardo Vega, and something was missing. I decided on another assumption, the most simple after Anne Terry herself—Ted Marshall. The most logical man in the case. Maybe it would lead me somewhere new.

I walked down Fourth Street in the crisp spring dusk. I got no answer to my ring at Marshall's apartment, and there was no light in the windows above. I tried Frank Madero. He was home. I went down through the basement. He stood aside to let me walk into his ascetic living room. He had been sitting in the dark, votive lights burning under all his crucifixes. He turned on the light for me. He was alone.

"Where's Ted Marshall, Frank?" I asked.

"I don't know. Maybe he go to the sister."

"Sarah Wiggen?"

"I think maybe. He say maybe he go."

He perched on the edge of one of his hard chairs like a woman in a tight skirt, alert and birdlike, but that was all. His act was way down. No, not an act. No more than a woman arching out her breasts with a man is an act, or a man being strong and gallant with a woman is an act. Those overt mannerisms need the proper stimulus, and so did his. I wasn't any stimulus. Maybe the votive lights of his religion held him down, or my continued presence—the normal public. Most homosexuals feel a little ashamed, and learn to hide. Our world has made them feel ashamed, taught them to hide.

"He needs a girl now," I said.

"They were friends, Mr. Fortune. They have bad time."

"Tragedy bringing them together?" I said.

"I see it many times," Frank Madero said.

"How close are you to Marshall, Frank?"

"Not that way, I said. Good friends."

"If he told you anything we don't know about Anne's death, you'd do him a favor by telling me. He'd do better going in on his own, Frank. He'll break sooner or later."

"He tell me nothing."

"Did you see him around here Saturday? Maybe with Anne?"

"Only Friday I see them."

"Friday? You're sure, Frank?" I sensed that I was rigid, like a vulture on a dead tree, alert. Was it going to be this simple? Such a small mistake? My brand-new assumption finding paydirt under the first rock? Why not? Most crimes are solved on trivial mistakes because no one knew, before it happened, that there would be a crime.

Neither Marshall nor Anne Terry aware that she was going to die, that for Marshall's sake they shouldn't be seen together on Friday.

Madero's eyelashes fluttered. "I think Friday."

"Be sure! What time on Friday?"

He was thinking. "The afternoon, I was not working. They was here, sure. But—maybe Thursday?"

"There's a hell of a difference, Frank."

He shrugged, helpless. "I think maybe Thursday."

He had said, first, Friday, and immediate thoughts are often right. After that I had scared him, made it too important. On the other hand people really don't remember small incidents well enough to say Thursday or Friday without going back and relating it to other incidents to fix the day.

"Was Mrs. Marshall with Anne this weekend?"

"I never see her with Anne no time."

"Okay, Frank, listen. If Ted arranged the abortion, you tell him it's better if he goes in on his own."

"Ted don't do that, but I tell him what you say."

Maybe I'm not a bad detective. If Ted Marshall was the man, then Ricardo Vega was clear, but I went up to the street eagerly. A good job was more important than my revenge. I went straight up to Anne Terry's apartment on Tenth Street. The happy fat woman super had changed her housedress for a robe, but the cigarette still hung from her mouth. The TV boomed behind her.

"No rest for the law, huh?" she said.

"I love my work," I said. "You said you knew some of Anne Terry's men friends. How about Ted Marshall?"

"Him, yeh. A boy. Nice, but weak, you know? She had to mother him. The kind that crawls inside a woman to be safe."

"Did you happen to see him last Friday?"

"Nope, not a hair."

"You're sure?"

"I said so, mister."

"So you wouldn't know if he'd been here or not?"

"Sure I'd know. He wasn't here. Least, not like usual."

"You'd know he *wasn't* here?"

She nodded. "Not like every Friday. I ain't missed him in almost a year, except last Friday."

"How? I mean, how did you always see him?"

"Because he always comes the same time: ten o'clock. I'm always out picking up the garbage cans after they been dumped. I watch TV until ten every morning, then I get the cans, and I been sayin' hello to that Marshall every Friday."

"But not this Friday?"

"Nope, and I'm out there a half hour at least."

A real lie? Marshall had told everyone that he had gone to Anne's apartment on Friday, as usual, and she hadn't been home. It was his whole proof that he knew nothing— he had expected Anne to be at home as usual, so, clearly, she had told him nothing. If he hadn't gone, then he had known that she wasn't home, and what more had he known or done?

I took a taxi uptown this time. Sarah Wiggen's downstairs door was open. I went up. There were voices behind her door. I recognized Ted Marshall's voice. My finger was on the doorbell when the tone of his voice stopped me. I listened. Muffled voices, Marshall and Sarah Wiggen, rising and fading.

". . . she wouldn't listen, Sarah. She had to do it. I was scared, but . . ." Ted Marshall's voice. Tragic, breaking as it rose higher; yet reluctant, jerky. ". . . she was so . . ."

". . . determined . . . always that way," Sarah's voice. ". . . challenge anyone, anything, when she made up her mind."

". . . didn't want to . . ." Marshall's voice with that odd jerkiness again, as if he was rocking where he sat. "Vega had me beat up, I couldn't fight . . . weak, that's me . . . I'd have married her . . . married all the time . . . those kids, God . . . I didn't know . . ."

"She destroyed things," Sarah's voice loud, a throb in it. Somehow, I knew she was holding his hand. "She didn't mean to, she just had to plunge ahead her own way."

I heard movement, a shuffling of bodies, and silence. Sarah's low voice seemed to mumble softly. Ted Marshall's voice had a kind of thin hope.

"We . . . we knew each other first, didn't we?" Marshall said.

Her voice was bitter, but thick, too. "She was more beautiful. You wanted her more. My body isn't the same, is it? Or is it? Tell me my body's as good."

Silence, and, "Christ, Sarah, you . . ."

"A live sister better than a dead one," she said. That combination, muffled through the door, of bitter edge and a drugged thickness. "Is my body good, Ted? Am I good —now?"

Movement on a creaking couch, and Marshall's voice lower. "I shouldn't even have come. I just . . . had to talk. What could I do? She forced me . . . damned pills . . . what do I do now? . . . finished, that's me . . ."

Silence. Sarah again, "I reported it to hurt you, both of you. I guess that means I still wanted you."

"God, Sarah, if we could, maybe I could . . ."

A soft thud and a rustle of clothing. I rang the doorbell. Time seemed to hang in the silent hall, and inside the room behind the door. Time suspended. I rang again. I could see them in my mind—close together, staring at the door.

"Open up," I called. "It's Dan Fortune."

Another silence, a whisper, and then she came and opened the door. Her hair was disheveled, her blouse open, her eyes smoky with the feel of a man's hands on her. I pushed past her. Ted Marshall sat on the couch, his shirt open at the collar, the shirt pulled out of his pants. He struggled into his jacket.

I stood facing him. "You never went to Anne's apartment on Friday. You were seen with her on Friday. You handled the abortion. I was listening at the door."

He was up and running at me. Like a blind bull charging. His weight caught me, his arm under my chin. I went over like a poleaxed steer. My head hit hard. For a moment I lay stunned. All black and green and red. When I struggled up, I could hear him running down the stairs. Sarah Wiggen stood pale, her hand in her mouth, her teeth biting her own hand. As I ran past her, her eyes were a battlefield of fear, desire, confusion.

In the street Marshall was half a block ahead and running. He was younger and faster. He reached the subway at Seventy-second Street a full block ahead. I plunged down the stairs, fumbled for a token, as the train came in. I made the door with a lunge. I chased through the cars. Once I had a glimpse of him far ahead, moving on through the cars. People sat in lethargy and stared at me as I ran past. Their eyes were curious, but not even their hands moved. The train pulled into Columbus Circle.

I had to decide—stay on, or get off? I got off. It was the wrong choice. The train was long gone before I gave up hope of finding him on the platform.

15

WHERE DOES a man run from his own guilt and panic? Unless he has planned an escape, he is inexorably pulled home, and I didn't think Ted Marshall had planned much for days. I could be wrong, but I had nowhere else to look anyway.

I went up and grabbed a taxi on Broadway. I watched the night city pass on the way downtown, and thought about Ted Marshall. The gaudy, sparkling blaze of Times Square with its masses of people mocked Ted Marshall in my mind. This was where he dreamed of finding his name emblazoned, but he had arranged an abortion, a girl had died, and now he was running. A man caught in a drama with no future for his name.

He had arranged the abortion, alone or not I didn't know. He had not known of Boone Terrell, or the house in Queens, so if he was alone in guilt, then her death had not been murder. Before I could know, I had to find him, talk to him.

A blind man running through the night city. No one lives in a smaller world than a city man. For a rural man his home is a whole town, an entire countryside. For a city man home is a neighborhood, a narrow world of a few blocks, a few friends. The rest of the giant city is as alien as a foreign country. All doors are closed, any stranger can be an enemy. There is nowhere to go, and a man in panic runs to what he knows. It was a theory, anyway. Terror seeks the familiar.

The taxi dropped me at Marshall's apartment house. I went to the rear. There was no light in Marshall's windows. I went down into the basement. Frank Madero's rooms were silent, no light under the door. I used my keys. Madero's apartment was empty, votive lights guttering eerily. I rode up to the Marshall apartment. I heard nothing inside, and opened the door.

The four rooms were dark; as still as a lunar landscape. Light from other buildings cast pools of faint light near the windows. I bumped into the overcrowded furniture, and found no sign of Ted Marshall in his own room. I went back out into the hall to see if there was a place to stake out. There wasn't. I was considering that a stake-out in the street would be better, when I heard an elevator coming up.

I ducked back into the dark apartment, and closed the door. I heard the movement behind me. I had time to see a large, dim shape, nothing more. I had come in from the light, and my eyes had not adjusted to the dark. His had. I took a slashing blow of something hard and metal. Only time to see the motion, try to evade, fail . . . on my knees, down but not out. My head split pain. I tried to get up. My brain told me I had to fall and roll away. Caught between the two commands, I did nothing. I kneeled like a prisoner about to put his head on the block.

A thick arm came around my throat. I tried to reach back with my lone hand. The arm tightened . . . squeezed . . . black . . .

I had two arms, a fine figure of a whole man. Two fine arms, and still couldn't evade her blows. She hit hard for a woman, Anne Terry: "I'm a good mother, Gunner. I love my kids, Gunner. I just want a chance." Why didn't she love me with my two fine arms? Sarah Wiggen's eyes smoked at the touch of hands on her breasts: "I saw him first. I love him. Hate her."

I opened my eyes. I saw nothing. God, I was blind! Doc, you never told me I'd be blind, blind . . .

Shapes emerged from a black pit. A ghostly furnace. Some . . . washtubs? Thick, square pipes over my head. The sound of traffic somewhere. People walking. The night sounds of the city. Where I sat nothing moved. Silence, dust.

My head ached, not badly. A small wound burned hot on my temple. My throat was bruised. My feet were tied, I saw them in the dim light where I sat against a wall. My hand was tied behind me: to my belt, and then to some kind of pipe. The furnace said I was in some cellar. If I had been unconscious for very long I would have felt much worse. So—I had not been carried far. The basement of Ted Marshall's building.

I tried my bonds. They wouldn't give. I couldn't move to find a way to cut them. I had no miracle escape tools.

I yelled.

I got an echo, and a pounding head. No one came.

I considered time: hit about 7:15, out for maybe ten minutes, so nearly 7:30 P.M. now. All at dinner, early TV.

I yelled anyway.

I began to know how a prisoner in solitary confinement feels. Time motionless.

Later, I decided to identify my attacker. Strong, quick, muscular—big? Run down the list, Fortune. Nuts. What did I remember? Maybe he was weak, slow and skinny. Surprise did it.

I yelled.

I dozed in the dim dust. Hours now, or a few minutes? What had he wanted? Not to be found in Ted Marshall's apartment? Urgent business with Ted Marshall, no outsiders wanted? Someone who had known about Queens, and knew what the right pills would do to Anne Terry?

I yelled.

A door opened above. "Hello? Someone down there?"

"Behind the furnace," I called.

He found me, stared. A round little man with vest and a watch chain. "What happened to you?"

"Practical joke. Get my hand loose."

He was nervous, shocked by the unusual, and his hands fumbled, but he made it. After he helped me untie my feet, he looked around for monsters in the shadows.

"Just a joke," I said, "but thanks."

"Sure," he said. He retreated quickly up the stairs.

I looked at my watch: 9:32. Two hours at least. I walked through the cellar toward the stairs, and saw a broad shaft of light from the direction of the superintendent's apartments. Frank Madero stood in his open doorway, peering in my direction. I walked to him.

"I hear someone yell," he said. "Just now. You?"

"Someone hit me, tied me down here. You didn't hear me yelling before?"

"I just come home."

"Ted Marshall here, Frank?"

"I don't see him since I talk to you."

I edged in past him. The votive lights still flickered, but the apartment was empty.

"I see a man maybe six-thirty, when I go out," Madero said. "Big man, blond. I think one of men who beat up Ted."

"Where?"

"Out front. Like he watch building, you know?"

I took the elevator to the fifth floor, and got out warily. I listened at Marshall's door. No sound, no light. I used my keys, and this time went in ready. When I was sure that the place was really empty, I turned on the light. I checked the closets of Ted Marshall's room. All his clothes seemed to be there, and three suitcases. No one had even sat on his bed.

In the living room I searched the floor where I had been hit. I found nothing. Then I saw the two glasses, and two cans of beer, on a coffee table. Both glasses were empty, ringed with dried foam. I had a sense memory of the coffee table being empty. I also remembered the pools of light from other buildings. The worn drapes were drawn now. All but one set open to a closed rear window. A chair near the undraped window was not on the marks it had made in the rug. I opened the window and looked down.

Down in the courtyard something black lay in stray light from other apartments. A bundle of old clothes. I left the light on as I went down in the elevator. The courtyard was slashed with beams of light from many windows. A concrete yard fenced with a cyclone fence, the gate locked. A chorus of TV words and music came from the apartments all around me in the night—the Greek chorus of mid-century America.

Ted Marshall lay on his back in the clothes I had last seen in Sarah Wiggen's apartment. One arm was broken under him. His neck was broken. What else was broken I couldn't tell, and the back of his head was crushed in a pool of blood. I saw no marks that couldn't have come from the fall. His pockets contained money, keys and a wallet. In the wallet there were a few credit cards, old newspaper clippings that told how good Ted Marshall had been in some stock company show, a lot of small portrait pictures of himself, and two nude pictures of Anne Terry. It was hard to remember she was dead. It was almost harder to remember that Ted Marshall had been alive.

I went up and called Gazzo.

Gazzo watched the Medical Examiner work. Detectives were all over the courtyard, and up in the apartment.

"Two hours in the cellar?" Gazzo said.

"While someone had a beer with Marshall."

"Nothing says they were the same: the visitor, the man who tapped you, and the killer. Marshall fixed up the abortion?"

"That's how it looks. But maybe not alone, with this."

"No suicide, Dan? You're so sure?"

"The window was closed. He didn't close it himself. So he wasn't alone."

"Men jump in front of friends," Gazzo mused. "The friend closed the window. Reflex. He could have hit the way he did from a jump."

"Why was I put on ice?"

"Him or the friend. He had to know you were after him after the Wiggen girl's place. Later, scared witless, he jumped. Where's the mother?"

"She works. Okay, if there was a friend here, why didn't he yell for help when Marshall jumped?"

"Maybe not a real friend. An associate. Someone who wanted no connection to Marshall, but not a killer."

"You want it to be suicide, Captain?"

"Sure I want it a suicide. Neat and simple," Gazzo said. "Abortion and suicide. What about it, Doc? Suicide?"

The M.E. stood up wiping his hands. "My guess is no. The autopsy may help. Dead about an hour, no more. He might have been hit first. A jump should have landed him farther out."

Gazzo nodded, thought for a time. "I guess I go back out to Queens and check Boone Terrell's story some more. That McBride was seen around, Dan?"

"The super said so."

A detective called down from above that Mrs. Marshall had been located at work, was on her way home. Gazzo went up. I left to put a band-aid on my cut temple.

Ricardo Vega's name was up above the show title on the marquee of The Music Box Theater on Forty-fifth Street. I went in through the front. The auditorium was dark, some thirty people scattered across the rows of orchestra seats watching the rehearsal on the stage. I slipped into a seat in the last row. Marty wasn't on the stage, Ricardo Vega was. In his sweat suit and boots, doing a scene. Most of the other players were in costume. It didn't matter to Ricardo Vega.

I didn't know what the scene was, but it was Vega's. He seemed taller, more powerful, and even in the sweat suit he gave a sense of dignity that made me feel suddenly calm. Calm and no longer in the theater. Almost without being aware of it I was no longer in a dark seat; somewhere else, sunk into the moment on the stage. His voice carried with no effort to all parts of the theater, encompassing the whole theater within his quiet voice. He moved with authority and a sense of joy. Totally alive. Transformed into something that was always Ricardo Vega, and more than Ricardo Vega. Something with a life of its own that was all of Ricardo Vega and much more. Not a different person, rearranged. Taken apart and put together in a different pattern—the pattern of the person he was creating up there in a world he made more real than the world where I sat. Oblivious to all but his art. Nothing held back, nothing left out, all of himself given, and more than himself. Given to the audience, but not for them, no. For his art, for his whole life. In his sweat suit he held us all in his work, the hands of his art.

Then it was gone. The orchestra started to play, and Vega began a dance, the chorus behind him. Began to caper like a wooden puppet, a smile on his face as false as his acting was true. I had forgotten in the suspended instant of his art that the show was a musical. I watched him, capering and vulgar, lost behind the plaster smile. Art turned to charade, the entertainment of burlesque—look, Ma, I'm popular! He began to sing, no music able to hide the sense of desperation in his voice.

When the scene was over, Vega stood with his head bent like a penitent as he listened to the music director.

I went backstage.

16

LAST REHEARSALS are worlds of private tension. Only the stage manager notices a stranger. I was lucky, the stage manager was setting a new scene. Marty's scene. I saw her alone in the wings, her lips moving as she paced, prepared. It was not a time to go to her. Art is one of the few things that can only be done alone, and yet can only reach its goal as the effort of a selfless group. Each artist must do his work alone for its own sake, for the truth of the work itself, and all artists must work together for the common whole, the final product for the world. Both together. The paradox of art, and maybe the paradox of life, too.

Ricardo Vega's dressing room was closest to the stage. Vega wasn't there. The business manager, George Lehman, was. He saw me in the narrow corridor. Heavy, solid, he came out with the short, quick steps of a small but thick man. A quick glide, as if on wheels, only the solid legs moving. His bald head glistened with sweat, and his suit was as wrinkled as ever over fat.

"You want something, Fortune?"

"Some talk with your boss," I said.

"He's busy. He's got no time to waste, okay?"

Without Ricardo Vega near he was a different man. The jumpy manner of a slave existing on the whim of the prince was gone. A kind of solid presence. He was his own man, too, and the fleshy face no longer seemed so flabby. He could not stop the sweat, mopped at his face and hands with a handkerchief, but there was that muscle I had seen before under the flesh, a solid jaw, a firmness to his eyes that watched me.

"Why don't you just mind your own business, Fortune? Leave Rey alone, you know?"

"He made himself my business, Lehman."

"The girl? A tramp actress? Come on, that kind flops for anyone, twice on Sunday. Why blame Rey for trying? You think he's the only one? Take a tip, watch that director, Kurt Reston."

"You know all about tramps?" I said.

"I wasn't always on top, mister. I did my time with tramps. I wouldn't spit on any of them. If it ain't Rey today, it's someone else tomorrow. Believe me. I know them all."

"You're on top now, Lehman?"

"That's right. Money, a home, a decent woman. Get a decent woman, Fortune, the kind you know what they're thinking when you're in bed with them. I've got two boys in college, a girl marrying a rabbi. My old man was a pushcart peddler in Brownsville. Rey did it for me. Leave him alone."

"All you have to do is eat his dirt," I said.

His thin-shell eyes were neither angry nor surprised. He had heard that charge before. He lived with it. All he did was mop the sweat from his hands.

"Brownsville is a bad place," he said. "Most guys never get out. They die in the gutter. I had my gutter, ran with a Jew gang worse than you could know. I took five-to-ten for armed robbery. I learned. You got to have money and respect. For ten years my kids wore patches and ate potatoes. Who wants an ex-con? Rey hired me. I'd learned accounting in prison, and for Rey I worked hard. My house is in Manhasset now, North Shore, right? You think I'll let tramps or their studs kick Rey? Stay out of this, Fortune. Find something else to play detective on."

"Stay out of it? Out of what, Lehman? You don't mean Marty. What's Vega mixed in I should stay out of?"

His face and eyes gave away nothing, but he was worried. He was tight inside. He mopped at his face. He seemed to be trying to decide just how much to say.

"If Rey lays off your woman, will that get you to stay out? Just walk away, forget it?"

"Forget what?"

"Just lay off! We can play rough, too. Be nice."

"What's so important now, Lehman? Maybe Ted Marshall?"

"A cheap punk who got what he deserved."

"Didn't the beating do the job? What more was there, Lehman? Did Marshall know more, do more, and Vega had to—"

A burst of loud music drowned me out. Lehman stopped listening, mopped at his face as the scene on stage ended, and the performers trooped off. Everyone grim, as only performers at late rehearsals can be grim, the girls half naked in their exercise tights, but somehow sexless. Marty came off, saw me, and came to take my arm, hold tight. Ricardo Vega was behind her.

"Well now, the gumshoe lover again," he said in his bantering tone, but his heart wasn't in it. His voice was strained, his eyes abstracted, the witty prince lying flat.

"I saw your scene," I said. "The song-and-dance, too."

Everything about him seemed to be far off, at a distance. Sean McBride appeared from somewhere, found a chair in the dressing room, straddled it. His limp eyes watched only Vega. He whistled between his teeth, made a paper bird with his big hands—a folded paper bird with wings and head that moved.

Vega said, "Everyone has to be George M. Cohan today. The voice of the people. You're a dance critic now, Fortune?"

"Ted Marshall was killed tonight," I said.

He paused, shrugged. "You play with blackmail, you get hurt. You expect me to care?"

"Is that a statement, Vega? Blackmailers get hurt?"

"Call it a proverb. Was there evidence I killed him, too?"

"You expected there would be?"

George Lehman said, "Rey was working here all night. I was with him. So were fifty other people."

"I only kill people between shows," Vega said. There was a strange bitterness in his voice. Odd, out of place.

"Lehman wants me to forget the case. I wonder why?"

"Look, Fortune, I'm tired. Take your girl and go, okay?"

"Where was McBride all night, Vega?"

Sean McBride worked his paper bird, watched only the bird and his hands. "Ask the lady, mister. Little Marty there."

I looked down at Marty. "He was with you, Mart?"

She dropped my arm. "When was Marshall killed?"

"Somewhere from nine to nine forty-five P.M.," I said.

"McBride left my place before nine. That's only a few blocks from where Marshall lives," Marty said.

Sean McBride shrugged. "I got me some drinks."

"Maybe he did," Marty said, a lightness in her voice that maybe only I recognized. A warning of trouble. "You've been sending him around to keep the pressure on me, right, Rey? Hints that you really like me, could send me places. Today I was busy—pictures, costumes, all that —but when I got home around seven tonight, Sean boy was waiting. Not for you, Rey, for himself. He wanted my precious body, the one I should hand around to show what fire I've got inside. He didn't offer me anything, no sir. He's a real man, not a tired old creep like you, Rey. He was doing me a favor. He doesn't have to buy a woman. He was sorry for me, stuck with a cripple and an old man. He doesn't think you can cut the mustard, Rey. He can, yes sir! An ox, and about as smart. I got him out short of being raped. That was a surprise. Maybe he went for drinks. Maybe he stops short of murder, but I wouldn't count on it."

She had drawn a crowd by now. The performers. Silent and uneasy, they didn't know where to look. I watched Marty. Lehman watched McBride. McBride watched only Vega. Vega stared at the floor, and I sensed something—he no longer cared about Marty. Something had pushed her from his mind. He raised his head.

"Pay McBride off, George."

McBride stood up. "Rey, I'm sorry, you know? She pushed—"

"Get him out of here!" Vega said. "I want him gone."

"I didn't say none of that, Rey! She's lying. A break, huh? Anything you want me to do."

Vega exploded in the dim backstage. "How much do I have to take? Hounded! It's got to stop! Christ, do I have to handle everything myself?"

He was in his dressing room, the door slammed shut, before anyone knew what he was doing. George Lehman blocked the way to the door. Sean McBride looked at Lehman, his face blank. Then he walked away out the stage door. Everyone drifted away, and Marty went for her mink.

McBride wasn't in sight when Marty and I left. We took a taxi to her apartment. McBride wasn't there either, and I breathed easier. Marty tossed her mink on a chair.

"Make me a drink," she said. "Triple martini."

She kicked off her shoes and vanished into the bedroom. I made the drinks. I stood with my whisky at the window. A cold night wind had come up, and the shadowy citizens hurried home. I thought of Paris five centuries ago, of François Villon scurrying through the night looking for a safe lodging in a city as wild as any savage land. Every man clawing for his needs.

Marty came out in her long, green robe. She curled with her drink at one end of her long couch. I took the other end.

She drank, shivered. "That animal McBride told me about the abortion, between grabs at me. He was sure Marshall had fixed the abortion. Now Marshall's dead. Suicide, Dan?"

"No. Ted Marshall maybe didn't do it all alone."

"Rey Vega?" she said. "I've been thinking, it doesn't seem right for Vega to do such a stupid thing, take such a risk."

"Important men, rich men, kill people. Not often in our world, they can get what they want easier ways. But it happens. Some intolerable pressure, some half-rational motive."

She drank. "McBride said someone was trying to involve Vega in it. Someone who wants to cause Vega trouble."

"Involve Vega? How, baby?"

"Just mix him in it publicly, I think. McBride said he might have to beat someone else. He was proud, thought it would make me swoon. Could it have been Marshall? McBride killed him?"

"Some new blackmail? Did he mention any name?"

"I had my mind on his hands. The pig!"

Her eyes were wide with a kind of pain. I moved to her, touched her arm. She shrank away.

"Don't, Dan! Not tonight. No man. I don't want the smell of a man. You understand, Dan."

"No," I said, "I don't understand."

"I just don't want any man near me tonight!"

"I'm not just any man, Mart. I'm me, Dan, and I don't understand, no. I shouldn't be 'any man' to you."

"I'm sorry, Dan. Not tonight."

"I'm sorry, too," I said.

I got my raincoat and left. She didn't look up. She curled tighter, her martini in her hands.

I walked for a long time in the sharp night wind. To the river. When you love a woman, want her, and she says no, a giant steel hand tears you up inside. You want to smash walls, and you understand why men kill for passion. I wasn't "any man" to her, I couldn't be or what was there, and I walked by the river for a long time before I turned into the first river saloon I found. I didn't even want to talk to Joe Harris, no. I had a double Irish. I began to calm. Sometimes I wonder what men who don't drink do when they are chopped up inside?

The Buddhists, Zen style, tell you that peace is found by leaving the world. They don't mean death, even if that is a kind of peace; they mean withdrawal. They mean not needing the world, learning how little a man needs to face himself with a smile. They mean hopping off the merry-go-round. I've tried it. I jumped off many times, and I never really got back on the last time. A middle-aged roustabout who dropped out and goes where his shoes take him. But it's not really part of our Western world, and no man escapes the world that made him. A Western man can't stare at a wall and find peace. We can get off the carousel, but the music goes on inside.

If you can't leave the world, and you don't have some simple belief to tell you what is right and wrong, there is only work. I had a case. For society it was a case worth nothing: two dead zeroes who had given the world little, and been worth less to the world. Knowing why they had died wasn't worth the time of one detective who should be out protecting decent people. Not to society, no. Yet Captain Gazzo would work on it, and so would I.

For two kids without even a weekend mother, yes, and just to do the job right. True, but more than that. For Anne Terry, who had wanted to give much to an indifferent world, and who had been worth a lot more than many. A girl, woman, who had kept the faith in her fashion, in the ways allowed to her with the pressures she had inside she could not help. A girl with the courage to carry her conflicting demands, and to dare for her dreams. She had made a mistake, but for a large dream, not for a small greed, and her presence filled the case like a hollow inside me. As if, somehow, my work could bring her back.

So I drank, and I worked. Ted Marshall had arranged the abortion. Maybe not alone, or maybe someone had come into the action for his own reasons. Someone who had killed Ted Marshall? Why? McBride for Vega? Maybe McBride on his own?

I drank, and I thought. At least, it took my mind off Marty and my need to be loved.

17

MY FIVE cold rooms and ready pot of coffee greeted me on a chill new morning. I had stayed sober, not called Marty, and lay looking at the thin sunlight without a hangover. I felt good.

I jumped out of bed, the chill sharp on my bare skin, and for an instant had the illusion of being far away. A hotel in Paris. A bed-sitter in Manchester. A flat in Stockholm. Out of some new bed to cross to a window and look out at the light over an alien city. A bright, new morning. Dazzling and new, and, because the city was strange, aware that someday there would be no new mornings for me, so each morning a complete life. For those who climb slowly from the bed they have always known, morning is only another day.

I had my coffee, and enjoyed the morning at the window, until New York became familiar again, and I called Marty. She never got up before noon if she could help it, so was asleep. She cursed me out, said she was all right, told me to call later, and hung up. I called Captain Gazzo. His female sergeant told me he was out. Sarah Wiggen didn't answer; she went to work earlier than a sometime detective.

I wore my old pea jacket when I went down to the diner for some breakfast, because I was still feeling the illusion of being somewhere else. Amsterdam, maybe, ready for a robust Dutch breakfast before a walk along the canals. The illusion held through pancakes, eggs and bacon. It finally faded as I walked downtown toward Ted Marshall's apartment house.

The lobby was spotless this time, almost shining. Scrubbed in deference to death, maybe, or maybe Frank Madero had needed to keep busy through his long night with a friend dead. Or was it the order of the owner; remove the marks of police boots, the evidence of murder in a proper building where murder didn't happen but had? There was a hush to the building, even the TV sounds muted. Real blood was more interesting. I could imagine the good wives working with ears cocked for new violence.

Mrs. Marshall answered the door. She wore a hat, and all black, and her face was round and motherly again as if her moment of battle was over. She looked now like those calm, silent old women I had seen in the war picking through the ruins after the battle had passed. No more worries, the curtain rung down on both fear and hope.

"Come in, Mr. Fortune."

"You're going out?" I said.

"To get him. The police have been kind. They don't . . . need him any longer."

Which meant that Ted Marshall had died from the fall and nothing else. Her voice had a soft texture, comforting. She sat down, so I sat. She got up.

"Tea? I'm having some," she said.

"Fine, thank you."

She sat down. "It won't be ready yet. I'm sorry."

"So am I, Mrs. Marshall, but I have to ask—"

It wasn't my voice she heard. "You were here last night? That Captain, Gazzo is it, he told me. I had to identify poor Theodore. My company let me go. A few days with pay."

"That's good," I said, feeling lame.

"You were here? You never saw Theodore?"

"No. Someone was in the apartment, I was hit. You have any idea who that could have been, Mrs. Marshall?"

"No," she said, heard her private dialogue. "I tried, you know? Poor Ted, he had such fantasies. Like his father. Most people assumed I doted on Theodore so because his father had been dull, ordinary. No, Theodore was exactly like his father. A handsome dreamer, weak, full of ambitions they hadn't the capacity for. I knew Anne would hurt him. She was a good girl in her way, but much too much for him."

"He arranged her abortion, Mrs. Marshall?"

She nodded. "I didn't ask him, but I knew. He was nervous that Friday. Saturday he was gone most of the day, and when he came home he was an awful wreck. Theodore never could face trouble. He was a boy who wanted the world to make a wide, sunny path for him with no gray days. After the police came the first time to ask him if he knew where she was, why she was missing, he was too frightened to move. He just lay there in his room. Only a boy, I so hated to see him frightened like that."

"Was anyone else mixed up with him, helping him with Anne? Did he talk about anyone special?"

"He never said anything to me, Mr. Fortune."

"Did you see him with anyone? Someone special, maybe? Some stranger to you?"

"I don't remember anyone, no."

"Can I look at his room?"

"Of course. The tea should be ready."

I searched Ted Marshall's room. The police had been ahead of me, and Gazzo does a complete job. I found no lead to anyone else, no clues. Only the closet full of clothes, all the best, and shelves of books, mostly plays. In the books one role in each play had been marked all through in the margins. The roles Ted Marshall had seen himself playing. All the plays were big plays, and all the marked roles were big roles—the male star. Nothing small for Ted Marshall.

In the living room Mrs. Marshall had the tea poured. I took a cup, sat down. She perched, drank her tea.

"You're continuing to investigate, Mr. Fortune?"

"So are the police. We'll find who killed him."

"It seems a sad kind of work. He's dead, who or why doesn't matter very much. I expect the reason won't make much sense. We live in a senseless, frightened world. Men who kill are always afraid. I'm not sure I want to know why Theodore made someone so afraid of him. I remember a play he did once. There was an old woman in the play whose son had been killed, and the son of a neighbor woman, fighting against each other. All the old woman could think was that the two women stood on each side of scales of sorrow, balanced by the bodies of the dead boys."

What did I say? In the silence of that musty apartment where she had worked for her son's weak dreams she seemed to be seeing the scales of sorrow, and all the dead boys. The doorbell rang without reaching her. I answered it for her. Frank Madero came in. He was pale and stiff in a Cuban-cut suit with a rakish nipped-in waist. The suit was too small for him, old and faded, with marks on the padded shoulders where it had hung for too long unused in a closet.

"It time we go, Mrs. Marshall. I got to work special," Madero said. There was a grayness to his dark face, a puffiness around his eyes as if he had been crying. "You find yet who kill Ted, Mr. Fortune?"

"Not yet. What about you? You heard, saw, nothing?"

"Only what I tell you last night. I come home just a little before I see you."

"Ted didn't come to you at all?"

"Maybe, but I'm not home, yes? He don't feel so good, I see that. I think maybe he knows about the girl, Anne, but I don't ask. He's my friend. If I am here last night, maybe he alive."

"You suspected he fixed the abortion for Anne?"

"That makes him a bad man? Because he help her? She makes the baby, she wants to stop baby. He do his best, yes?"

Mrs. Marshall had her coat on. "I'm ready, Frank. Will the funeral parlor people be there?"

"I just call them to go," Madero said.

Together they walked to the door. She seemed to have forgotten that it was her apartment. She was leaving me in the room as if I lived there, not her. She looked back at me.

"In that play Theodore did there were a lot of old women with dead sons; a civil war of some kind. At the end the old heroine goes for her son's body. She'd seen the first of him, she said, she'd see the last of him. What was the pain she suffered bringing him into the world, to the pain she was suffering carrying him out of the world? She didn't care what had killed him. Once he was dead, the reason didn't matter."

She went out leaning on Frank Madero—as Juno Boyle had at the end of the play she remembered. *Juno and the Paycock*, O'Casey. A little war and a cheap murder. Is there a difference? You tell me, I don't know.

I gave them a few minutes. Then I went down. I wasn't feeling good anymore in the clear, cool day. When I found why Ted Marshall had died, it probably wouldn't make much sense. About as much sense as Juno Boyle's civil war. Or as much sense as the isolation inside us all that made Marty shrink in her anger even from me.

The new morning had come down to just another day. I stopped in O. Henry's for an Irish. It was too early, but my sense of clean well-being had gone with the morning. To ease my guilt before I had a second, I called Gazzo again. The lady sergeant had a message this time. If I called I could go to an address on Hudson Street. Gazzo had left the message only an hour ago, the place wasn't seven blocks from O. Henry's.

Police cars were out front when I got there. One of a row of tall old-law tenements with the fire escapes in front, and terra-cotta decoration all over the grimy brick façade. Small shops on the street level ranged from grubby *bodegas* to elegant antique emporiums. Three levels of patrolmen passed me up to the second-floor rear apartment. A railroad flat, the dark rooms smelling of sweat, cooking, rot and urine. All the rooms were bare and empty except the kitchen.

In the kitchen was a white enamel table, two stained straight chairs, a water heater, a sink, and the usual high bathtub with an enamel cover to make a work area. The walls and fixtures had that thick, leprous look that comes in New York flats from endless years of paint—layer on layer. Detectives worked and crawled all over the room. Gazzo stood watching. Lieutenant Denniken from Queens was with him.

"You know Denniken, Dan," Gazzo said.

"Fortune," Denniken acknowledged, and nothing more. He walked away.

"What is this, Gazzo?" I said.

"Where the abortion was done, Dan. Cleaned, but not good enough. Blood under the tub, broken syringe needle, traces of hair and maybe foetal matter. Lab has it all now."

I looked around the barren rooms and felt sick.

"How'd you find it?"

"Remember Boone Terrell saying Anne had something written down in case Vega couldn't meet her? Last night, after we found Ted Marshall, I told Denniken to go over that Queens house with a sieve. We had luck. Denniken had a brainstorm—the little kids had cleaned, all right, but they couldn't carry out the big garbage cans. Denniken found the note deep in the garbage. This address, and Vega's name."

"But I heard Ted Marshall admit it all."

"All, Dan? Or just part? I figure the beating he took did more than shut him up. I think he changed sides. A Judas goat for Vega. That's why he got killed; he knew too much."

Gazzo moodily watched one of his men taking apart the sink drain, another taking fingerprints. "I see it that she had a bigger club over Vega than he let on. That's what was missing. He paid her off. Then he fixed the abortion. Maybe he told her he wanted it safe, or maybe that he wanted to make sure she kept her bargain. What he really wanted was his payoff back, and to make sure she stayed silent—permanent."

"Murder?" I said.

"I read murder, but to prove it we'd need the quack who did the job. The only other weak link is dead—Marshall. Maybe we can pin Marshall on him somehow. If not, and he doesn't break, I guess it's the abortion charge. He was here."

"I want to like it," I said, and I did, "but a man like Vega needs a life-and-death motive for murder."

"Who says what's life and death to any man? Any man can kill under the right pressures, conditions. How many times have you said those things yourself, Dan?"

How many times had I said them? All true. I had at least implied them to Marty only last night.

"Besides, there's still the abortion," Gazzo said.

"What places him here personally, beside the note? Who rents the flat?"

"Vacant. The super swears he knows nothing. We're working on him, but it doesn't matter. We found this, Dan. In a pile of rags and junk near a lone chair in the next room —sort of a waiting room, I guess."

He handed it to me. A silver money clip, initialed: R.V. On the back was an inscription, worn down: *To Rey, a coming star: Applause!—1-20-50.* A well-used money clip.

Gazzo said, "It's Tiffany, easy to check. You know, in thirty years you learn that people are funny, they have small quirks almost as unique as fingerprints. It looks like Vega leaves bits of jewelry around."

I said, "Marty says he thinks he's being involved in it all by someone who wants to give him public trouble."

"This is more than some trouble," Gazzo said. "He's tied to the girl. He's got motive already. He's placed here now. He's got no alibi for Saturday—we checked after Boone Terrell's story. Terrell's story is the final nail, and there are small hints from everyone. The D.A. does a dance with what we have."

"Can I see that note Anne had?"

It was typed, not written. Gazzo saw my startled face.

"Look at the back," he said.

The paper was a page from one of Anne Terry's production plans for her theater. There were handwritten additions to prove it was Anne's. A discarded page? It was garbage-stained, but it looked like a correct page, and I couldn't remember seeing any discarded scrap pages in her desk.

Gazzo said, "Sometimes the plain and simple is just that."

A neat woman, Anne Terry, orderly. This page rang a bell. Did I remember seeing it? Was Anne a woman to take a page from her files and use it as scrap? On Friday, or Thursday it would have been. Some pages had been missing on Tuesday. But on Monday? The first time I'd looked? No. I was sure. Or was I? If I was, how did I prove it? Vega said someone was involving him. I saw a shadow, a man at Anne's desk and files on Tuesday. Emory Foster, a "friend" of Sarah Wiggen.

18

THIS IS the age of magical technology. Detectives use all the modern tools of science, yes they do. I used a basic tool in a drugstore on Bank Street—the telephone book. It's simple when you know what to look for. No Emory Foster was listed, not in five boroughs. No one has ever invented a free-lance writer without a telephone, or a poor free-lance writer with an unlisted number.

I called Sarah Wiggen. She didn't answer. She worked somewhere. Who had said it? Ted Marshall, yes—Sarah worked in some kind of residence hall for females. That could take all day. I flagged down a taxi on Hudson Street. The day was hotter now near noon, and they were still playing soccer in the park. Silent men scoring imaginary goals in make-believe important contests because they had nothing better to do in the richest country in the world.

The superintendent of Sarah Wiggen's brownstone had the steady eyes of a Corsican bandit.

"Yeh?"

"Sarah Wiggen isn't at home. You know where she works?"

"Why?"

"I'm working on her sister's murder. I need her."

He thought about it. "Columbia University. The Mary Higgens House. It's in the book."

I found another drugstore. At The Mary Higgens House they passed me along the line until I reached a crisp female voice of uncertain age who had to be the boss. I explained who I was, and what I wanted. She thought about it, too.

"I see," she said at last. "Sarah said that if we needed her she would be at home, or at her sister's apartment."

I thanked her, and went out for another taxi. This time the cab went through the park. The soccer players had ended their match, and sat on the grass looking as if no one had won. They looked as if they thought that no one could win. Men have to have more than themselves to live for, something they can believe will go on after them. It doesn't matter if it's true, only that they believe it. Children and money aren't enough, especially money. That is what the solid core of our nation doesn't understand, and that is why we are in trouble.

At Anne Terry's apartment the buzzer answered my ring. Upstairs, Sarah Wiggen had the door open, was working over a floor full of cardboard boxes. Her hair hung in her eyes, and she wore slacks and an old sweater that made her look more alive. She hadn't touched the files as far as I could see.

"Where do they go?" I asked, nodding at the boxes.

She brushed the hair from her eyes. A soft gesture that raises a woman's breasts gently. "I went over to see them, Sally Anne and Aggy. Do all children talk so much, I wonder? They were all over me: Aunt Sarah. Sally Anne talked about her mother. She said she'd have to take care of her father. Little Aggy moves her arms and legs just to watch them move. They're so alive, aren't they? It makes you happy."

"Sad, too," I said. "You're taking these things out?"

"What they want. I bought toys, too."

"Are you taking her files?"

"No."

I went to the files. The page with the typed note on the back was missing. It had not been replaced with a revised page. Maybe the police had taken a revised page, but I thought not.

"Why not take the files, her papers?"

"Who would I give them to?" It was her first reference to Ted Marshall. She looked out a window. "You heard last night? Of course you did. Am I that hungry, frustrated? I suppose I am. I wanted his hands on me. Anne, alive or dead, just didn't matter. What he had done didn't matter, or what he was: weak. I hated Anne, didn't I? Because men wanted to take her, and who wanted to take me? If he came back to me, I'd have won."

"Maybe it's good," I said. "We go on that way."

"I can feel his hands in my mind, but his hands can't feel anything," she said. "Who killed him, Mr. Fortune?"

"I'm working on it," I said. "Who's Emory Foster, Sarah?"

"What?" She packed an ash tray. "A friend, I told you."

"No," I said. "It came to me, you call him *Mr.* Foster. Yesterday you sent him here, no, he offered to come here for you, and when I saw you around six P.M., he should have been back with you, but he wasn't. Who is he, Sarah?"

"I call him *Mister* because he's old."

She went on packing, but there was a change—the pleasure was gone. She had been mobile, talking, and now I saw the stiff reluctance in her where she knelt packing. She had been open, and she had closed.

I said, "When you first reported Anne missing, you didn't mention Ricardo Vega. You've told me you went to the police to make trouble for Ted Marshall, you were sure Marshall was the man involved. You didn't care about Vega—your own words, Sarah. Next day, you suddenly did tell the police about Vega. After Emory Foster had come to you?"

It was a question. She didn't answer, so I went on. "I don't think you knew Ricardo Vega existed, Sarah. Not as Anne's lover. You weren't close to Anne; she kept her life very secret. That was her way. You only knew about Ted Marshall because she took him from you. You never met Emory Foster before Monday. He came to you the way I did—he read the news story."

She stopped her packing now, but she didn't look up. "All right, yes, he read the paper, he wanted to help find Anne. He came to ask if I knew about Ricardo Vega. I didn't know, so he told me, and I told the police. That's all."

"Help find Anne? He never heard of Anne. Why come to a total stranger, you, to help find another stranger?"

"You came!"

"Yes," I said, "I came. Why did I come? I owed Anne something, I'm a trained detective, but was that my real reason? No, I came to try to get Vega! I think Emory Foster did the same—with a big difference. I called you Monday night, remember? Someone was with you. I told you I was going to Anne's apartment—coming here. I found Anne later that night. Was Foster with you? You just happened to mention where I was going?"

Her head was down, hair dangling like a curtain over her face, as if too much weight rested on her neck. She didn't seem worried, or evasive, only reluctant, being made to do something she didn't want to do. Her voice was unfriendly.

"He was there, yes. I might have mentioned you."

"And he left right away?"

"I don't remember."

"Do you know his real name?"

"Foster is the name he told me."

"How do I find him, Sarah?"

"I don't know. You proved I hardly know him."

"He would have given you a way to contact him. I'll find him, Sarah, but I'm in a hurry. You want more killing, maybe?"

She was sullen. "I've got an address at home, somewhere."

"Let's go," I said.

She got her coat to cover her old clothes, and we went down for a taxi. We rode in silence. The driver took the West Side highway to avoid the lunch-time traffic. The river was high with the spring flow, cleaner, and some rusty big ships blew steam and water and looked happy now that winter was over. Sarah Wiggen watched the river, and the big ships straining for the open sea, and maybe that changed her mood.

"Have you ever felt purged?" she said.

"I don't know, maybe."

"Cleaned out?" she said. "Brain and body purged clean. When they told me Ted was dead, it seemed to clean me out inside. Last night I was like a starving female mouth: all flesh, thick. Today I feel all space. Clean, and far apart in a wide sky as if Anne and Ted had never been part of me. I feel . . . free."

"You were in love with Marshall?"

She considered it. "I wanted him to love me and not Anne. That's all I can say. When he dropped me, I quit everything."

"For him?"

"My excuse, yes. The truth is I didn't have what it takes," she said. She looked away from the river toward midtown and the theater district we were passing. "I was getting nowhere in the theater. No one hired me, said I was good. Anne used to say that if you haven't given up, you haven't failed. I don't know what it takes to never quit, never accept any judgment except your own. Courage, or arrogance, or stupidity, maybe, but I don't have it. It's not in me."

"Anne had it, yes," I said. I could see her standing in the rain, alone, only herself.

"She had the abortion because she wouldn't give up, settle for less than she had to have. The arrogance, or courage, or stupidity to risk all the way," Sarah said, still watching the indifferent city spread out in the spring sun. "I'll live all my life knowing I settled for less. You don't marry a house in New Rochelle without always knowing that all you have is less than you wanted. I'm a smaller person than my sister. Possibly even a better person, but smaller. I don't think I can fool myself that anything I do now will matter very much."

"But you'll try hard to fool yourself," I said. "Like the rest of us, you'll want what you do to matter a lot."

"I'll probably even succeed," she said, "but not all the time."

She was still a colorless girl, without any snap, but I liked her better. Unless she was fooling herself, and me, all the way. She had something on her mind as the taxi dropped us at her brownstone. She climbed up to her bleak apartment as if pushing through some thick liquid.

Inside, she rummaged in her desk without taking her coat off. She handed me a slip of paper with an address on it: 422 East Eighty-third

Street. There was a telephone number. I had no need for it, but I took it. I didn't want her warning Foster. She might know the number, but I didn't think so.

"Emory Foster couldn't have done anything to Anne, could he?" she said. "What good will it do to find him?"

"There's Ted Marshall," I said. "I don't know what Foster's done. I know the police think Ricardo Vega got them both killed, and I'm not so sure anymore."

"The police think Vega did it all?"

"At the moment."

She held her coat tight around her, and her face was abstracted, thinking. I couldn't tell if her thoughts were worried or happy. A new thought came to me.

"Sarah, how did Boone Terrell know where you lived? Had he been here before?"

"What?" she said, blinked. "I don't know. I suppose Anne told him. I'd never even met him, I told you that."

"So you did," I said.

"Can't you leave Boone and the children alone?"

I left her standing there angry. She didn't hate her sister or Ted Marshall anymore. Hate was still a strong emotion in this world, and it was easy to stop hating the dead.

19

EAST EIGHTY-THIRD STREET, as far east as 422, is Yorkville —the big German section. Famous for *sauerbraten* and beer halls where you can dance cheap, the *Bund* was popular here just before the war, and a lot of the local citizenry still think we fought the wrong enemy in that war. (Not that right-wing Germans are the only ones who think that in this country.) There are sub-minorities, too, mostly Czech and Hungarian.

Number 422 was another old-law tenement with the fire escape in front, but built of grimy gray-stone without even the terra-cotta decoration. Instead of a *bodega*, the grocery store on the street level had a sign in Magyar. I paid off my cabbie, and climbed the steps to the vestibule. There was no Emory Foster listed on the corroded mailboxes, but there was an Emory Foxx. The name was on an engraved business card, yellow with age, in the box for 4-B. A telephone number had been crossed out—a Los Angeles number, Hollywood.

The "B" apartments on each floor were just at the top of the stairs to the left. I rang at 4-B. I waited. I was looking forward to the look on Emory Foster's, or Emory Foxx's, face when he saw me. I was disappointed. At my second ring there was a shuffling inside, and the door opened on a thin, gray-haired woman in an old black dress. She wore jewelry everywhere—costume jewelry in gold and silver and stones of every color. Her eyes were glazed, and her feet were in ragged slippers. She just stood.

"Mrs. Foxx?" I asked. "Is Emory home?"

She looked at me.

"Is Emory a heavy man, maybe fifty, has a tweed jacket with elbow patches? He's a writer?"

"Why?"

"I'm looking for him. About Ricardo Vega."

She nodded. "Emory should be back soon."

She shuffled back into the apartment. I went in. It was a railroad flat, with those same thick-painted walls from the generations of painting by tenants who didn't have the energy to strip the old paint before they put on the new. Paint, instead of scrubbing, to cover dirt. The furniture was like Emory Foster, or Foxx, himself—good, but old, and out of place where it was. It was in Spanish style, heavy and velvet, and had probably once graced more spacious rooms. The living room itself was a hothouse, with two electric heaters going. Plants hung and stood everywhere. There were bowls of goldfish by the dozens.

"Emory knew Vega in Hollywood?" I asked.

She didn't answer. She had sat down in a plum velvet armchair, picked up a tumbler of thick, brown liquid that had to be sherry, and gone back to what she had been doing—reading a thick historical novel with a voluptuous cover of a raunchy cavalier in padded tights, and a costumed lady with bursting breasts.

"How long has he known Vega?" I asked.

"Too long."

She didn't look up. I didn't really exist. Nothing did. Just her tumbler of sherry, and the broad-shouldered cavaliers, and perfumed breasts, of centuries ago.

"Why does he want to pin murder on Vega?"

She looked up, but not at me. "I hope Rey Vega dies in jail. Just dies. That much, at least. Dead and buried."

She thought about that for a moment, then went back to her book. It was all unreal, like seeing a mental patient sitting alone in some sanitarium room, reading an imaginary book.

"Dead and buried," I said, prompted.

Her eyes up again, still looking at something only in her mind. "He buried us, but he forgot to kill us first. We're dead, but we can't lie down."

"How long, Mrs. Foxx? Why?"

Back to her book. I wondered if she even knew when Foxx would be home? The hothouse room was making me sweat, or maybe it wasn't the heat. I had to get out. Emory Foxx, if he was framing Ricardo Vega, wasn't doing it all alone. Boone Terrell had to be part of it, maybe Sarah Wiggen. Mrs. Foxx didn't even notice me leave, lost in the reality of Louis the Fourteenth.

In the hall it was like returning from the past, and going down the steps in the sun was like coming back to life. The apartment upstairs made me think of that tiny room in The Bronx where Leon Trotsky had sat alone and dreamed of murdering the Czar and living in the halls of the Kremlin. Trotsky had done it.

Once out, I crossed the street and headed for the avenue and the nearest subway to Queens. I saw the messenger out of the corner of my eye. In a messenger's uniform, but there was something familiar despite the uniform and the military cap. He went up the steps of number 422. Another man went into the building behind the messenger. Together? I couldn't tell. Two women went up the steps at almost the same time, all mixed together.

I waited across the street in front of a corset shop, its small signs in both German and Czech. I didn't have to wait long, and I had my answer when my wait ended. Maybe five minutes. The second man, not the messenger, came out of number 422, and stood for a moment on the steps: George Lehman, the business manager of Ricardo Vega. The messenger had been Sean McBride. Lehman stood on the steps in a topcoat with a velvet collar, and looked up and down the street. Then he came down and started across the street to my side. I turned to study the display of corsets in the window. Out of the corner of my eye I saw Lehman take up a position in front of a German bookstore. He continued to look alertly in both directions. I saw his instant shock when he saw me. He stood rigid as if trying to decide whether I had seen him or not. I concentrated on the corsets. When I looked again, Lehman had crossed the street again, and was already half a block away.

I went after him. Ahead he went around the corner onto the avenue. When I reached the corner in a sprint, he was invisible among the throng of afternoon people. A taxi pulled away from the curb. He could have been in it, but it had green lights all the way. I went back to number 422. I went in, and climbed up to the fourth floor. I slowed, stepped softly as I reached the top of . . . lifted and flung like a feather . . .

. . . an illusion—the door of 4-B bent out like a bow, flying past to crash into the opposite wall . . .

. . . a giant hand crushed at my chest, lifted me, hurled me in mid-air backwards and flailing in empty space . . .

. . . *Crump! . . . Wooooosshh* . . .

. . . wall of air . . . smoke . . . debris . . . burning . . .

BANG! . . . ear-splitting . . .

. . . halfway down the stairs, bounced . . . rolled like a giant pinwheel . . . smashed a wall on the floor down . . .

I knew an explosion when one hit me. How many times at sea in the war? Exploding, the whole ship hurled up and out into black water . . .

A thing, smoking and burning. At the top of the stairs. A man? . . . One arm, half a face, half of one leg, smoking cloth hanging in pieces, strips . . . a "thing" falling . . . one enormous eye with a look that wasn't pain or hate or anger or . . .

. . . Oh . . . the pain . . . Oh . . .

There were dreams.

A burning man with half a face and one eye with a mild look, reproachful, "Now what did you want to go and do that to me for, world? It's not fair, you know?" Did I know that half-face?

A heavy face, florid, and thick shoulders bent over to look into my eyes. "Fortune . . . Fortune . . . What . . ."

Something blue . . . dark blue . . . something white . . . wail of sirens . . . black slickers . . .

Dreams—and my mind clear the instant I opened my eyes.

Clear, crystal sharp.

I had been bombed. Yes. I was in a hospital room. Yes. I had been blown up. Yes.

Marty sat reading a book in the dim light. I watched her. Awake, my mind clear. Clear in terror. I whimpered.

"Dan?" Marty put down her book.

I said, "Tell me."

"What, darling! Tell you what, Dan?"

She stood beside the bed, touched my right shoulder. Why? Why not hold my . . . hand?

"Tell me," I said. "My . . . my . . ."

"It's all right!" She understood. "It's all right, Dan." I felt her fingers on my hand. "Your arm is fine, Dan."

It was there. My arm. My one arm. My one-and-only-thank-God-arm! Sweat poured into my eyes. I giggled. I shook. I laughed. Someone called for a nurse . . .

The second time I woke up sunlight blinded me.

"Close that damned shade."

Sunlight cut off. Orange juice, and my face and throat seemed to be all there. I wondered what hospital it was? I didn't really give a damn.

"Drink it all now, that's a good boy."

The juice went. I lay back and closed my eyes. I thought of all the hospitals I'd been in. How nice it was to lie and think of the other men out on the cold seas with storms, and submarines, and mines, and sharks, and weary work. I dozed. I felt peaceful.

There were two doctors and three nurses.

"Well, how do you feel?" one doctor said.

"Pleasant," I said. I decided to spend my life in bed.

"Don't you want to know what day it is?"

"No," I said.

"They always want to know that first," the doctor said.

"Okay. What day is it?"

"Friday afternoon. Two days, but you're okay now."

I don't know when they left. I was thinking how nice it was to doze and not have to do anything, think of anything.

On Saturday I ate breakfast and lunch and saw the city outside. Time came back. It always does.

"What's the report, Doc?" I asked.

"A concussion, no fracture. A wound on your head. Two broken ribs, torn ligaments and muscles in your left leg. Bruises all over. Some wood splinters. All-in-all, lucky. You should go home on Monday or Tuesday."

"Have I had visitors besides Miss Adair?"

A nurse said, "A Captain Gazzo, and a Joe Harris."

"Who was killed by the bomb?"

"Two people, I think," the doctor said. "I'm not sure."

I dozed. I'm one of those people who bring books to a hospital, but never read. I go over in my mind all the places I've been in my life, places that are always alive for me. Maybe because in a hospital death has to be kept away.

But death, like time, comes back, and with it all the busy, important schemes and tactics and drives of life.

That bomb had not been meant for me.

20

A BOMB meant for Emory Foxx, alias Emory Foster. I thought about it all Sunday morning.

When health returns, all the needs return, too; good and bad. Maybe the only time in his life that a man sees what is really important is when he's sick, or dying—sun, time, and being alive with everyone else alive. I was feeling normal, back in the world with my today-and-tomorrow desires, demands. I wanted Ricardo Vega guilty of something. Now I was sure he was. That bomb had been intended to kill Emory Foxx.

I thought about it all morning, fiercely, and in the afternoon Marty came. She had a tall, fair, handsome man with her. A man I didn't know, who wore good, quiet clothes, and had a nice smile.

"Hello, baby," Marty said. "Kurt came along; we're doing some scene work. Dan Fortune, our director Kurt Reston."

Kurt Reston had a firm grip, but not too firm since I was a sick man. He made easy small talk, then faded into the background. A confident man. Probably good at his work.

"You scared me this time, Dan," Marty said.

"Who was killed?" I asked.

"Sean McBride, and a Mrs. Emory Foxx."

So I really had known the half-faced "thing" at the top of those stairs. Sean McBride, wondering in his last seconds why the world had gone and done such a thing to him. And Mrs. Foxx, sure: the innocent bystander, who, from the glimpse I'd had of her, had died inside a long time ago from standing by while Emory Foxx hated Ricardo Vega. Now she'd taken his bomb.

"They've arrested Vega," Marty said. "We've suspended."

"What's Vega charged with? Did they arrest Emory Foxx?"

"That's all I know, Dan. We're being paid while we wait. George Lehman's running things. Kurt has a new show for next year I may have a part in. We're working on it."

"Very good, baby," I said.

She talked some more about what she was doing, and kissed me before she left. Kurt Reston held the door for her. He had the manners not to touch even her arm while I could still see them. My one and only real friend, Joe Harris, came in next. We talked about nothing for an hour. Joe is that kind of old friend. He was just glad I was alive.

Captain Gazzo finally arrived about 5:00 P.M. He had a two-day growth of whiskers on his tender face, and his eyes had that steel surface that comes from long sessions of talking around and around a case.

He lighted a cigarette. "Ten seconds earlier and you're dead. Homemade bomb, a stinking fuse job. The damn fool."

His hands shook on the cigarette. It had to be fatigue; Gazzo has no nerves.

"Sean McBride took the bomb there?"

Gazzo nodded. "We found the makings in his room. Bomb squad tells it like this: McBride wore a messenger's uniform, had the bomb in a package. Must have told the wife he had to see Emory Foxx in person, and waited. Foxx was late—he got there right after it blew, found you down on the third floor."

"Yeh," I said. "I remember seeing his face—vaguely."

"When McBride heard you coming up, he must have figured it was Foxx. He gave the package to Mrs. Foxx, and went to open the door. That's when it blew. It has to figure like that: the woman was in pieces, she had to be holding the bomb. McBride lived a couple of minutes and staggered out."

"Ricardo Vega sent him with the bomb? To get Foxx?"

Gazzo blew smoke. "McBride never met Emory Foxx. But Vega and Foxx have been enemies for maybe thirteen years."

"So you're holding Vega. What does he say?"

"He says Emory Foxx framed him for Anne Terry's death, and maybe for Ted Marshall's murder. He says he knows nothing about McBride and the bomb. Says he'd fired McBride."

"He had," I said. "I was there."

"Sure," Gazzo said. "Maybe he wanted you to hear him fire McBride. Or maybe he cooled down, kissed and made up. Vega's got the reputation for blowing up fast, cooling down fast. Artistic temperament. Remember when he told us he hadn't sent McBride to Anne Terry's apartment the day you saw McBride there, and McBride got picked up by us?"

"I remember. Vega said he had no reason to send McBride."

"He didn't have a reason, not logically, but Ricardo Vega seems to work to his own logic," Gazzo said dryly.

I could believe that—the prince makes his own logic.

"Now he admits he did send McBride to Anne Terry's place that day," Gazzo said. "He'd read the newspaper, and we'd talked to him a little, so he sent McBride to find out what was up, and to keep him out of it. A little private investigation to cover himself just in case. He had McBride keep an eye on everyone just to know what was what. Then after you described 'Emory Foster' when we were at his place, he knew that Emory Foxx was involved, and sent McBride around to find out what Foxx was doing. All that he admits—but no bomb!"

"Yeh," I said, thought in the bed. "If it's true, Vega dug himself in deep by trying to be too smart, too arrogant."

"If it's true," Gazzo said.

"What's Emory Foxx's story?"

"He admits to hating Vega. He says he knew Anne Terry was a Vega girl friend. When he read she was missing, he went to Sarah Wiggen and told her about Vega. After that he snooped around, watched Vega, watched Ted Marshall, talked to Boone Terrell. He hoped to prove that Vega handled the abortion. He thinks Vega found out, and sent McBride to kill him."

"Does he say why they're enemies? So long?"

"The D.A. won't talk about that, not even to me. He says it's a bombshell motive. The kind juries believe."

"Won't Vega tell what it is?"

"Not a word. Refuses to discuss Emory Foxx, except to say the man was framing him. The lawyers have Vega clammed up, too. They don't want him denying things he won't be charged with. Juries have a way of remembering denials."

"How does the D.A. see it all?"

In sunlight Gazzo seemed smaller, drier. Night was his life. "Vega paid the blackmail to Anne Terry, but just to lull her. With Ted Marshall's help, he fixed the abortion. He murdered her with the wrong pills, probably by letting Marshall give them to her so she'd think it was okay. He had McBride kill Marshall to silence him. Emory Foxx was snooping too much, found out too much, so Vega sent McBride with the bomb."

"What did Foxx find out that was too much?"

"He says he saw McBride at Marshall's building just before Marshall took his dive, among other things. Mostly he backs up what we know—says he saw Marshall and Vega talking on Tuesday, saw McBride skulking around you, Marshall, Anne's apartment. The money clip traced to Vega, by the way. He claims he lost the clip five or six years ago."

I knew what the D.A. would do with a money clip lost six years ago that turned up in an abortion room where evidence already placed Ricardo Vega.

"Version number two," Gazzo said. "Vega did it all the same, except that he didn't murder Anne Terry. It was a bungled abortion. Once she was dead, Vega panicked and covered with two murders. The D.A. likes that better. With Marshall dead, unless we find the abortionist, we can't tie Vega to the pills. A bungled abortion, covered by murder, is the kind of panic a jury understands. They can see themselves doing that."

I let it all sink in for time. Gazzo seemed to be doing the same.

"You don't like either version, Dan?" Gazzo said.

"I'm sure that the note was a plant." I told him why. "Probably the money clip, too, but I can't prove it."

"Maybe they were, especially the note," Gazzo said, "but that doesn't clear Vega. Lieutenant Denniken is up for a commendation on Vega. Denniken points out that maybe the note is a plant, but that doesn't make Boone Terrell a liar. Vega was the man, and Anne told Boone, but there wasn't any proof. Emory Foxx talked to Terrell, heard what Anne had said, and made up the note to back it up."

"I think it was a frame-up all the way," I said. "That's why Vega sent McBride with the bomb."

He crushed out his cigarette. "Prove it, Dan. Maybe I see it the same, but I'm blocked. Chief McGuire says I have to give him one solid piece of proof it was a frame-up before he'll let me put taxpayer's time into busting a good case. I could work on my own time, but a Homicide Captain out of his own territory doesn't blend into the background, and Denniken's out to hog-tie me. The D.A.'s convinced, too —Vega's guilty of the abortion. I think he's guilty, too, Dan, but I want it to be the right crime. Go and get me the right crime."

I thought about it for the rest of the night—alone. Sometimes lack of knowledge can help a man see better. An expert, like Denniken and the D.A., rarely see that things can be different than they are. An aura of inevitability hangs over the judgment of experts—what is, must be. They can't see beyond their own experience. I can, sometimes.

Now I could see Boone Terrell in the Interrogation Room—too firm, too contained, too calm. Like a man holding in his grief because he had work to do. Money work, maybe—paid to tell a false story. Money work for his children.

Or maybe Boone Terrell just wanted to hurt Ricardo Vega. And maybe, in the end, he had—if he had lied, and that lie had made Vega send a bomb to Emory Foxx.

21

THE HOSPITAL let me out at 4:30 P.M. on Monday. My ribs ached, I limped, and my hat wouldn't have fit if I'd worn a hat, but I could have been another victim. I felt good.

I cabbed home, got my old .45 caliber revolver, my duffle coat for the night, and took the subway to Long Island City. I rode the same bus I had the night I found Anne Terry in the house on Steiner Street where the two smallest victims waited for her to wake up. This time I stopped first at The Pyramid bar. I had an Irish. It still tasted fine.

"You know Boone Terrell?" I asked the bartender.

"Sure do," he said. "You a cop?"

"Insurance adjuster," I said. People like to help other people get insurance money, beat the big company. "Terrell needs a man he says was in here looking for him on Monday night. Heavy man, red-faced," and I described Emory Foxx.

"I remember, sure. He come in after the cops was here. Talked to Matt Boyle, a pal of Boone's. You want Matt?"

"Later, maybe," I said.

In the daylight the semi-detached houses on the quiet streets looked neither individual nor manipulated. Anonymous houses, unimportant, like the homes of all the faceless billions on earth at any given moment. At the house on Steiner Street there was loud music again from inside. When I rang, the same small, running feet answered like an echo.

"Hello, it's you," Sally Anne said. "My Mommy's dead."

Behind her, the smaller girl, Aggy, wailed in fury because her sister had answered the door first.

"Be quiet, baby," Sally Anne commanded. "You want my Daddy? He's home."

What I wanted was to walk away, leave it alone. At least I think I did. I hope I did. What happened to Ricardo Vega, and justice, didn't matter, no. Let him go to jail on a frame, or go free on a bombing. Let these little girls have what they could get. I hope I wanted to walk away, even if I couldn't.

"Can I come in, then, Sally Anne?" I said.

"Aunt Sarah's here," little Aggy said, needing to have her share of me. "Aunt Sarah's nice like Mommy."

The barren living room was still grim, but it no longer had the look of children playing house. A woman's hand was obvious, and Sarah Wiggen sat on a sagging couch. She watched me as I came in. Boone Terrell was beside her, still wearing work clothes. I suppose he was comfortable in them. They were together, yet somehow apart, as if they had been waiting for me—waiting for someone, or something. Terrell spoke gently to the two little girls.

"You go hear your music now."

Aggy ran out. I saw her fall onto a pillow in front of the record player in the middle room. Sally Anne perched on a chair, determined to stay with the grownups. Maybe she was afraid inside that if she lost sight of her father, and her new-found aunt, they, too, would go to sleep and not wake up.

"Go on now, honey," Terrell said.

Reluctant, the little girl backed from the room. Visitors had not been happy events in her life of late. Boone Terrell watched her for some seconds after she had gone. Then he looked at me. His gaunt face had that faint smile I had seen before on the faces of big, slow men in rural towns. Calm and alert behind quiet, flat eyes.

"You come out to talk with me, Mr. Fortune?"

"Perhaps he wants me, Boone," Sarah Wiggen said. "Did you find Emory Foster, Mr. Fortune?"

"In a way," I said. "Someone tried to murder him. You didn't hear about it?"

"No," she said. "I hardly knew him, and Boone didn't know him. Your head! Were you—?"

"I got too close," I said, and said, "You didn't want me to talk to him, did you, Sarah?"

"You think I tried to—!?"

Boone Terrell said, "Sarah's been with us most all the time since Wednesday. The funeral was Thursday."

"Here?" I said. "Since Wednesday? All day?"

"I took my vacation to stay with Boone and the children for a time," Sarah said. "Boone has to find work now."

"I didn't know he could," I said.

"I expect it won't be so easy," Terrell said.

"It takes money to raise children," I said.

"I expect how it does," he said.

Sarah said, "I intend to help out for a time."

"That should be fine, then," I said, "with what Emory Foxx paid Boone for that story."

Almost anyone can tell a lie, talk a whole concocted story, and lie to a series of questions if ready. It takes more skill, practice, to lie with silence, with your face, to a direct statement. It's even harder for most of us if we have been waiting for the accusation, knowing it would come, but not sure just when. Sarah Wiggen couldn't do it. She looked down at her hands, her fingers twisting like worms. Boone Terrell was better.

"I guess I don't rightly understand you, Mr. Fortune," he said. "Who would that Emory Foxx be now?"

Nothing changed in his gaunt face. The same small smile and flat eyes. All he needed was a stick to whittle.

"Emory Foxx is Emory Foster," I said, "and the man who 'helped' Sarah, and paid you to tell what Anne said about Vega."

"You got the advantage of me," Terrell said.

I had been standing. Now I sat on one of his half-hearted home-made chairs. "Boone, right now you've only signed a false statement.

That's bad enough. If you tell it in court, that's perjury. You want your kids to lose you, too?"

"I told what Annie said. Maybe it's true, maybe not."

"She didn't tell you Vega arranged it," I said. "There wasn't any note. Foxx planted it. Foxx did more to frame Vega. You want Vega to be charged for what he didn't do, and when it comes out, go to prison with Emory Foxx?"

"He got Annie pregnant," Terrell said. "She died."

"Did he kill her, Boone?"

"That depends how you see it, don't it?"

The small smile was gone from his rocky face now. His jaw muscles stood out like crags. He looked only at me.

"Maybe it does," I said. "Maybe Vega is guilty in a way, but what about Emory Foxx? A man out to murder Vega by using you, me, the law. That's what he's doing, Boone. Three more people are dead because of his actions. Nobodies like you, and me, and Sarah, caught between Vega and Emory Foxx. Vega started it by being what he is, but Emory Foxx carried it on, and you helped by lying for money."

Terrell said nothing. Rural people are less complex than the abstract city men, and more complex. They respect principle and truth, will fight for it, but they live in a world that respects values even more. They are rarely abstract. Tradition before universal principle and justice; family before truth; country before right; honor before fact. Truth is good, the clan comes first. Morality, yes, but defend the family.

I said, leaned, my coat still on and the big cannon heavy in the pocket where I hoped it would stay, "Boone, you don't have a choice. I know enough now to make your story smell even to Lieutenant Denniken. Sarah told Foxx how to find me Monday night, and he followed me out here. He found Anne dead. Somehow he found The Pyramid, and your friend Matt Boyle, and then he found you. Maybe he made you believe Ricardo Vega had gotten Anne killed, I don't know, but he paid you to tell that story of what she said about Vega. He was only muddying then, sniping at Vega, but then he found where the abortion had been done, and it got serious. He planted the note out here, planted evidence against Vega in that abortion room, and now it was bad. Foxx was lucky, the timing worked right, and Vega helped him a lot by sending Sean McBride around to snoop and watch—Vega looked like a worried man. The police have swallowed it, they have to the way it stands, but it won't hold. You're in trouble now, Boone, but if you go in on your own, expose Foxx, I think it'll go a lot easier for you."

Terrell hadn't moved a hair while I talked. Sarah Wiggen was watching him. His small smile didn't return to his gaunt face. He sat there like a rebel in the dock braced for torture, monolithic in his stubbornness. His eyes looked toward the inner room where the little girls lay wrapped in ragged blankets and listened to their music, colored cartoon books.

"Boone? " Sarah Wiggen said.

Terrell was impassive. "Easy on me, but I ain't got much chance workin'. The kids is young, they forget me. I don't say you got any part right, but say it's so and I tell it, I got to give up any money, right? Now, if'n I hold to what I told, maybe they say I'm lyin' and I go to jail, but I says there wasn't no money. Foxx he got no proof there was."

"They'll find the money, Boone," I said.

"Money looks kind of the same. I figure I could work out something for the kids."

Sarah said, "Boone, no. Not both of you. Children need what they know, someone they love, a parent."

"How much could it be, Terrell?" I said. "Foxx isn't rich. How long would it last for them? And later?"

He considered us both. Without expression. He could have been deciding what meat to have for dinner. A farmer thinking about whether or not to take his wife to town on Saturday night. He folded his hands in his lap.

"Since you got most already," he said. "What you say I should do?"

Sarah Wiggen held his arm in both hands. He didn't look at her, he looked steadily at me.

"First tell me what did happen with Foxx," I said.

"Foster, he called himself," Terrell said. "Like you had it, he follered you, found Annie. He watched you and the cops. When you all left here, he called Sarah."

Sarah said, "The police called me, and told me what had happened, that it had been an abortion. They couldn't find Boone; they wanted family identification. Foster, or Foxx I suppose, called before I left for Queens. I told him."

"So he found out it was an abortion," I said.

Terrell said, "He went an' asked neighbors, got told about The Pyramid. My buddies only told the cops what they got to. Foster, Foxx you say, talked money, so Matt Boyle told him better. He found me 'bout morning. Made his proposition."

"You took it," I said, "for the kids."

He moved for the first time. He leaned forward, clasped his big hands. "Maybe I done it for me. How was we livin'? Annie gone and all. Her money was what we lived on mostly. What was gonna happen to me? The kids, sure, and I was scared, too, and maybe I was hatin' that Vega. I knew the kid was his. I took it, cash money he got. He told me go to Sarah and make the story hold up. You was there, that's all."

"What really happened Friday, Boone?"

He squeezed his big hands. "Mostly like I told the first time. She come early, the whole thing with Vega'd gone bad. We was all going down to Carolina, for a while anyways. She was sick of everything, all them men. Not before Monday, though, 'cause she had to take care of the way she was. I guess I'd kind of figured the kid maybe was mine, so I got mad. She got mad back. The kid was Vega's, she wasn't having it no matter. Vega wouldn't do nothin' for her, not even help her fix it. Her partner in that theater of hers was fixin' her up with some kind of special Doc he knew about for Saturday. So I walked out and got drunk. Maybe if I'd stayed . . ."

He left it hanging, and so did I.

"Ted Marshall arranged it, paid for it?" I said. "You did know about Marshall?"

"I knew. I guess he paid; she didn't have money."

"You didn't know where she had it done?"

"She never said."

"Then how did Emory Foxx find out?"

They both shook their heads, sat silent. I stood up.

"All right, go in to Captain Gazzo, Boone. On your own, and to Gazzo at Centre Street. Take the money."

Boone Terrell nodded. "He gets off, that Vega. He didn't even help her. Maybe if he pays for it, she don't die. He got the money for a real doctor. He could of helped."

"Maybe he won't get off, Boone," I said.

His head went all the way down, and he was crying. His clenched hands against his forehead. Sarah Wiggen was up, came at me with her hands out to push me from the room.

"You got what you wanted," she said, her face white. "We were wrong, now go away! He can't stand any more. The money for the children, that's what kept him going, a purpose. He's got nothing to think about now but Anne."

I went.

22

MANHASSET IS on the North Shore of Long Island just outside the city limits. I took a cab from Steiner Street to Flushing Main Street, and caught the Long Island Railroad. From there it was twenty minutes on a slow train. Most of the trains are slow, and I had time to look out the window at the neat suburban houses on their manicured plots of small land. I had time to think of Boone Terrell who had been sustained by the need to act for his children, but who had now lost that need to act, and so had only Anne Terry to think about—his loss and his emptiness. Any life was better than no life, and a weekend wife better than no wife at all.

I had time on the slow train to think of Anne Terry, too. Somehow, she was fading in the inexorable twists of events. Her death usurped by the stronger hates of Emory Foxx and Ricardo Vega, as her life had been ruled by their power. She was fading among the neat houses outside the train window—the homes of people she had not known, and who did not want to know her.

Manhasset was exclusive once, a place of the rich. It's middle-class now, but still a nice place to live. Part of the exodus from the cities, the middle-class migration to a narrow safety that is not particularly Protestant, and not necessarily Anglo-Saxon, but that is very much white. A sterile landscape behind an invisible stockade of fear and power and advantage, built to keep out the poor and crude, the dirty and disadvantaged, the communal and bleeding. In these homes of the comfortable, the people want no intrusion, no competition. They want to keep the advantages they have, and Anne Terry could count for nothing here —alive or dead.

Anne Terry had had no dream of privilege, but only of work, of finding somewhere a reason to live. In this dark landscape they could only hate her for the wind she brought to shake their comfort, and she was fading from me among the Vegas and Foxxes and manicured lawns. I didn't want to lose her. I needed her with me among these houses that sat like impervious toads. I needed her honesty and her laugh: "I wanted something big, Gunner, you believe it. I made a bad play, a mistake, but I wanted it alive, Gunner man, not small and wrinkled and flat."

She was my reason, Anne Terry, and at Manhasset station I took a mini-bus taxi that dropped me at a red brick house with a lawn and lighted windows. The lawn wasn't especially large, and the backyard was fenced. A middle-class house on a well-behaved street in the quiet suburbs. If there were private quirks, they were firmly inside. Not even a careless gardening tool marred the proper order.

George Lehman opened the door himself. His suit coat was off, but he still wore his tie. A napkin in his belt, a black *yamalke* skullcap on his bald head that gave his fleshy face a kind of ancient dignity. He nodded to me before I could speak.

"Fortune, sure," he said. "Come in."

A small entrance hall was crowded, spotless, and smelled of rich food. The living room had that mixture of German and Russian heaviness of the New York Yiddish culture— dark, thick furniture; ornate silver *menorahs*, faintly oriental tapestries like *ikons*. In the dining room six people sat silent around a long oak table that gleamed white and silver, and an ornate samovar steamed on a side table. The six people were three male, three female. The males wore the same black *yamalkes*.

"My family," George Lehman said.

His fleshy hand moved a few inches. As if that was a command, all six people at the table stood and formed a kind of line in front of the table. The three males stood stiffly, the women with more diffidence. Lehman looked at me with what I could only call a soft pride.

"Mr. Fortune came to see me on business," Lehman said. It was a statement and an explanation, as if in this house George Lehman made the decisions, but everyone was entitled to know the basis of those decisions.

He indicated the family ranged in front of me one at a time with his thick hand. His voice different here, that gentle pride, firm but kind.

"My son Saul, he goes to Brandeis University."

A tall, thin youth with a dark beard, who bowed his neck.

"My son David. David is at Columbia University."

Fatter and shorter, like his father, David grinned.

"My daughter Sylvia. Soon she marries her rabbi."

The girl was petulant, but she hid it carefully. Her father not all she wanted, but she didn't say that in this house.

"My brother Maurice."

An older man, short, who smiled from a friendly face.

"My sister-in-law Sophie, who lives with us."

The poor relation, grateful, and admiring Lehman.

"And my wife Florrie. My best luck."

The wife blushed. "George, you embarrass your friend."

Lehman smiled, and I nodded to them all, managed a mumble. Only the oldest boy stared at my arm. Lehman dropped his napkin onto the table.

"You all finish dinner," he said. "Save some tea."

"I'll bring down two glasses," the wife said.

"That's fine, Florrie," Lehman said.

He nodded me from the dining room. Not even the wife had asked who or what I was, or why I was there. In this house George Lehman was the patriarch, benign and respected, never questioned. He led me down into the basement. It was a finished basement—playroom with pool table, refrigerator, television, record player, posters, the trimmings of young people; and an office with desk and leather chairs.

"Okay, Fortune, sit down," Lehman said.

He sat behind the desk, I took a chair. I still wore my duffle coat. He hadn't asked me to take it off. He had closed the office door. Upstairs, the patriarch with his family in his home. Down here, alone with me, the visitor from another world, he was Ricardo Vega's business manager.

He took off the *yamalke*. "We say prayers at meals."

"A nice family," I said. "Does Vega come here much?"

"Rey never comes here."

I heard a tone in his voice—Rey Vega didn't come here; Rey Vega would pollute this house, this family. The split identity so many of us live with today. Anne Terry had not been alone in living two lives, but where she had been one person in two, even three, sub-worlds, Lehman was two people in one big world. Anne was unique, to herself. Lehman was all too common these days. The work identity, and the private identity: separate, lost from each other. The private standards left at home, the public man with different values. The kind patriarch tall at home, moral, and the narrow servant of Rey Vega at work, flexible.

"You were hurt," he said, looking at my head.

"I was hurt," I said. "Sean McBride was hurt more, and Vega's in jail."

"A mistake. Rey didn't kill anyone."

"I know," I said, "Emory Foxx framed him good."

I watched his heavy face. His wary eyes, like thin shell, showed nothing, but his heavy eyebrows went up.

"You know that?" he said.

"I can prove it now, Lehman. I've got the proof."

"You? What proof? Foxx hasn't talked, I know him."

"First tell me about Emory Foxx. Why does he hate Vega? Fifteen years of hating, Captain Gazzo says."

"Nothing much to tell," Lehman said. "Just an old feud. Started before I was business manager. I was Rey's accountant then."

"The D.A. thinks a jury'll lap it up," I said. "You don't want to tell me?"

He mopped at his face with a handkerchief, shrugged. "They worked together out in Hollywood then. Emory Foxx was a pretty big writer at the studio. Rey was called out to do his first picture after dazzling them with those two big hits on Broadway. They worked together on the picture. They couldn't get along; it was Rey's picture, from one of the plays on Broadway. Foxx was running dry, played out, I guess,

142

and Rey was the new King. Foxx got fired, or shifted to another picture, actually. Pretty soon after that everyone got called up by one of those Congressional investigations."

I could see the sweat circles spreading under his arms in his shirt sleeves. He mopped at his hands. "It was happening all over in those days. Everyone hauled to Washington, or before a junketing committee on a witch-hunt. They called Rey. He told them straight: he'd been a kid Communist in Cuba, joined left-wing fronts later in New York— everyone had at the time. He'd busted years before, and he proved it. Emory Foxx clammed up, refused to talk. He got cited, went to jail for over a year, and got blacklisted from movies and Broadway. He said Rey 'got' him to ruin him, climb over him. That was crazy, everyone knew it. Rey was already in solid, on his way up, and Foxx had been dropped from the picture six months before. Rey didn't have any reason to hurt Foxx, none."

"How did he say Vega 'got' him?" I said.

"He never did say straight out, because he had nothing to say," Lehman said, angry. "The guy was a Communist, that's all. He was one then, and they knew he was lying, and he's still a Communist! Maybe that's why he's after Rey, because Rey's been against the Communists for years. Or maybe he just cracked crazy. I don't know, but he's been hounding Rey ever since he got out of jail—thirteen years, more! Hounding him!"

"No one seems to know much about it?"

"Because Foxx never come out in the open with it. All behind-the-scenes, private sniping, lying to people! He's too scared to try it in the open. Years ago Rey had to send lawyers to threaten slander suits, or libel. Foxx was on parole a while, and Rey warned him he'd charge him and send him back. No newspaper or magazine'll touch Foxx, they know Rey would ruin them. Maybe he's had it hard. I guess he finally cracked open."

When he finished, he sat for a moment as if seeing those old days. His face didn't look like the memory was beautiful. He moved, lighted a cigarette, waited for me to speak.

I said, "I guess he finally 'got' Vega, too."

He dropped the barely smoked cigarette into an ash tray, leaned across the desk toward me.

"You said you could prove it was a frame-up?"

"I can prove Foxx framed Vega for Anne Terry's death, maybe for Marshall's killing, but Vega had to try to murder Emory Foxx, and kill Mrs. Foxx by mistake."

I slipped my hand into my pocket, gripped my old pistol. I didn't think I'd need it, not really, but I like to be careful. A one-armed man needs help in a fight.

I said, "Vega sent Sean McBride. You know he did, Lehman."

I had my cannon on its way out. I never did see where his gun came from. A small automatic, maybe a 7.65-mm. Mauser, in his right hand. He held it at me. I brought my hand out empty.

"You saw me at Foxx's place," he said. "I wasn't sure."

A mistake, that's what I'd made. No, two mistakes. I had been sure George Lehman didn't use guns, few people do. I had been sure he wouldn't defend Ricardo Vega so far. Too many mistakes for my work. Inside, I was jelly, but I talked.

"I won't move anywhere, Lehman. You'll have to shoot here with your family upstairs, or nowhere. I'm tied to this case, Gazzo'll trace me to you easy. For what, Lehman? For Rey Vega? You and McBride were tools. You weren't even in the actual bombing. Turn witness for the state, you'll get off light. Vega's the killer. Kill me, you'll get caught, rot in—"

"What if Rey never sent us?" he said. "On our own."

We all make too many mistakes, every day. Most of them don't kill us. A third mistake—because all along I'd wanted Vega to be guilty of a crime? Lehman was saying that Ricardo Vega had killed no one, and he had a gun, and deep down I knew he was telling the truth. I was cold. I felt the chill down to my feet. My mouth as dry as caked mud inside.

Lehman said, "An ex-con's nightmare is going back. So I waited. If they were going to convict Rey for Anne Terry, why hang myself?

But you tell me you can prove Rey's been framed, and you saw me on that street, so now I have to move. You're sure you can prove Rey was framed for Anne Terry?"

I managed a nod.

"And Ted Marshall?"

I nodded again.

"You'll swear you saw me—across the street? Outside?"

Somehow, maybe it was his calm eyes, I sensed what he wanted me to say. The truth. "I saw you. Outside."

He nodded. "I could shoot you, keep quiet, maybe be safe, maybe not," he said. "It doesn't matter anyway. If I kill you, tell nothing, Rey Vega's going to jail. No jury could see it any way except Vega at least sent McBride to kill Foxx, any more than you and the police did. If I let you go and don't tell my story, it's even worse for Rey— he sent both of us. Maybe if you hadn't seen me—" He thought about that, shook his head as if wondering about himself. "Give me the pistol, Fortune."

He emptied my old gun one-handed, put the bullets in his pocket, the gun in his belt. He laid his automatic on the desk.

"I couldn't let you take me in," he said. "I go on my own. That way maybe they believe it all, maybe I get a break."

The saliva began to flow in my mouth again.

"Funny," Lehman said. "Right now I don't care a damn about Rey Vega. I'll lose all he gave me, anyway."

"What happened at Emory Foxx's place, Lehman?"

He had more on his mind. "I've been thinking all week. I'll never be important—no leader, no boss. I'm not hard enough to put my mistakes on the shoulders of another guy, let him take the punishment for me. Vega can. Big man. He'll wash his hands of me. I still have to tell it. A born loser, Fortune. Soft, scared to hurt another man. Hang myself first, and hope for a pat on the back."

He was right, but, somehow, his face didn't seem so flabby to me anymore. We'd both never be big men in this world. We didn't have the gall, the narrow ego to think that only we really mattered, counted for anything.

I called Gazzo's office. The night sergeant said that Gazzo was out picking up Emory Foxx. Boone Terrell was there. When I hung up, Lehman had his coats on.

"Why would you kill Foxx on your own, Lehman?" I asked.

"Not me," he said, "McBride. Let's go, get it over."

23

A WET NIGHT mist had moved in over the city as Lehman and I walked into Centre Street Headquarters. They told us Gazzo was in the Interrogation Room. Lehman had stopped talking soon after we left the subway. He walked like a man wrapped in years of silence.

Sarah Wiggen sat on a bench near Gazzo's office, the two little girls, Sally Anne and Aggy, asleep on blankets on either side of her. One of her hands rested on each of them in the midnight corridor.

"I wanted to be here," she said. "They'll sleep."

In the Interrogation Room where Boone Terrell had first told his paid-up story, and where some long ago loser would say how sorry he was as long as the walls lasted, Captain Gazzo and his silent team of shadows in shirts stood around in their casual poses. Boone Terrell sat under the light at the bare table. Emory Foxx had been put in a chair just at the edge of the light facing Terrell, with two shirts-and-shoulder-holsters behind him. Gazzo looked at George Lehman as we came in.

"Terrell's just telling us an interesting story, isn't he, Mr. Foxx?" Gazzo said.

Emory Foxx didn't answer. He wore a pin-striped suit coat this time, with baggy corduroy trousers and another expensive checked wool shirt. Now that I knew, he looked like what he was—a man who had been high on the well-paid hog once, and who still wore the rag-tag remains of those big days. His buffalo-face was still florid, but his eyes were battered, and his heavy shoulders seemed to want to sag.

"Okay, go on, Terrell," Gazzo said.

George Lehman stepped toward the Captain.

"Hold it, Lehman," Gazzo said, waved Lehman off.

"I want you to know I'm here on my own," Lehman said.

"You'll get your turn," Gazzo said. "Terrell."

Boone Terrell went on. He'd gotten to where Emory Foxx found him Tuesday morning. He handed Gazzo the money in an envelope, and then told what had really happened on Steiner Street the Friday Anne Terry came home early.

"I guess what I done wasn't so legal," Terrell said when he finished. "I guess I got somethin' coming."

"We'll talk about it," Gazzo said. "I think I want to hear what Mr. Foxx has to say."

Emory Foxx said, "He's lying, that's all."

"That's the best you can do?" Gazzo said.

Emory Foxx said, "His word, that's all you have."

Gazzo put his foot on a chair, leaned on his knee, stared straight at Emory Foxx. The thick writer didn't blink, stared back. Gazzo rubbed the stubble on his acid-sensitive face.

"No, we've got more than that, Foxx," he said. "The trouble with a frame-up is that it's like propaganda. As long as you believe it, everything sounds fine. The first time you don't believe it, everything falls apart. Fortune, there, he's got it all down better than us right now."

I moved into the light. I don't like interrogation rooms; they are where men are broken to less than men, frightened and alone, but this time I didn't feel too bad. Emory Foxx was another of those who think that only they matter, only his revenge counted. The unblinking toads on their dry rocks.

"Sarah Wiggen will tell how you came to her, a stranger, to 'help' a woman you'd never met. She'll say she told you where I was Monday night, and you left to follow me. You did, out to Steiner Street. You called Sarah, and she told you Anne had died, and how. You tracked Terrell through The Pyramid bar."

Gazzo said, "Terrell told us most of it before we got you, Foxx. Lieutenant Denniken already talked to the neighbors, to Matt Boyle.

He says you wanted Terrell, you talked money. We check your bank tomorrow."

"That note," I said. "I saw you at Anne's when you got the paper to type it on. I know that sheet was there on Monday. Anne Terry was orderly, she wouldn't have used a page from her plans. That was clumsy, Foxx, too risky."

"With Terrell talking, and Fortune's story, the note's proof against you," Gazzo said. "It's like that with a frame-up. A jury'll believe Vega lost the money clip now, too. That Hudson Street room checked out: her blood type, her hair, one thumbprint. Prints all over, none Vega's. How'd you know, Foxx?"

"Only Ted Marshall knew the place," I said.

"So you killed Marshall, too?" Gazzo said.

Emory Foxx had been sitting tall as if resisting a wall falling on him. Now he moved his head, a sharp negative.

"I don't murder people. That's Vega," Foxx said. He pressed his hands down on his knees. "All right, yes. I waited thirteen years for the chance. Thirteen years! Waiting; watching Rey Vega."

The silent detectives waited stonily, a small incident in their lives of wives, kids, a home in Brooklyn. Lehman showed cold fury, and Boone Terrell his calm impassiveness. Only Gazzo and I breathed hard. A moment of confession is like seeing a man cut open. Foxx looked up at us, his face almost proud.

"I knew everything Vega did, where he went. Thirteen years I've watched him. Every chance I could."

The pride faded. Maybe he was thinking of those thirteen years, and saw his wife in her costume jewelry from gaudier days. A woman lost in romantic novels, indoor plants, and goldfish, dead because of his obsession.

"I went to Sarah to at least make trouble," he said. "Then there was the abortion. It was my chance. Maybe I couldn't make it work, but it was a chance. I'd saved money while we rotted, just for when I might need it against Vega. I'd carried that money clip ever since I found it five years ago."

Gazzo said, "Marshall told you where the abortion was done?"

"You hit me?" I asked. "Tied me in that cellar?"

"Yes," he nodded. "When I paid Terrell to tell you Anne had implicated Vega, it was just a story. I had him mention a note to make it sound better. Then I realized I could maybe plant a note out in Queens. It was late, but it might work, evidence is missed the first time, sometimes. So I went and got that page from her plans, and started looking for Marshall. He didn't move out of that apartment with his mother until she left for work. When he came out, I lost him. So I waited in his place. I had to know where the abortion was done to write the note. Fortune came first, I had to hit him."

He sneered. "Marshall showed up just then. When he saw Fortune tied up, he was scared out of his wits. He was eager to help me. He jumped at the chance to blame anyone but himself. We carried Fortune to the cellar, but Marshall was ready to crack. He kept telling me it was an accident, they'd made a mistake. So he told me where it had been done, and I went and planted the money clip. Then I went out to Queens, typed the note on that page I had, and planted it in the garbage."

"What time did you leave Marshall?" Gazzo asked.

"I had to calm him, he was breaking up. He might have blown the whole thing. So we talked some. I suppose it was just after eight-thirty. I saw Sean McBride again. He had been outside the building when I went in, but inside when I left. He didn't know me, then, but I knew him. He must have been watching Marshall. When I left, the super was threatening to call the police if McBride didn't stop loitering around the lobby. I could see McBride didn't like being warned, but he left. He must have come back. He killed Marshall for Vega, just as he tried to kill me for Vega! But he didn't kill me, he killed my wife, and I'll see Vega burn!"

His voice had risen, almost happy in its intense hatred. Triumph was all over his heavy, buffalo face, eager in his thick body dressed in the remains of his days of success. He had been a prince of success, too, an important writer who was paid well, and he had waited thirteen years for revenge. But he wasn't a prince any more, just another victim now.

"Rey Vega didn't send McBride," George Lehman said.

Gazzo didn't look at Lehman, he looked at me. I nodded. Lehman took my pistol from his pocket, gave it to Gazzo with the bullets.

"No one brought me in. I could have run, Captain," Lehman said. "I came in to clear Rey Vega. I was with McBride when he took that bomb to Foxx's place."

"He was there, Captain," I said. "I saw him that day."

Gazzo held my gun. "You didn't tell me, Dan."

"Not until I had all of it," I said.

Gazzo turned to Lehman. "You might as well give us your yarn. Go on, tell me Vega didn't do anything."

"He didn't," George Lehman said. In his velvet-collared topcoat, immaculate white shirt and Broadway tie, he was all wrong in the dim room. But he was the ex-con, he knew what he was doing. "It was all McBride alone."

He looked for a cigarette in his pockets, found one. He lighted it. His movements businesslike as if talking to some clients. "After Vega found out from Fortune that Emory Foxx was mixed in the thing, he blew his top. 'Wasn't he ever to get rid of Foxx? Wasn't there any way to stop Foxx short of killing him? God, he wanted it finished with Foxx, over, ended!' Like that, more than once. Raging. You know how he talks, Fortune. 'Did he have to handle everything himself?'—all that. Just blowing steam, the way he always does. It's the tension."

He smoked, spread his fleshy, soft hands out in disbelief. "That McBride was half-nuts, at least. After Rey fired him he begged me to help him get back in good. He'd lost his big chance playing the fool. I like people; I'd helped guys Rey was mad at before. Rey cools quick, sometimes. So I tried. Rey said what good was Sean McBride to him? I told McBride. I figured that was the end. Only it wasn't. McBride came around to the office. I was out, so he left a note—my secretary saw him write it, and I've got it here. He said he was going to do Rey a favor by handling Emory Foxx, he wanted me to help."

Here he stopped again. His face had a distant look, as if seeing how it had all happened. "I knew how much Foxx had driven Rey crazy over the years. This time it was worse, and even the show was going bad." He looked at Gazzo. "Right then I heard you'd pulled Rey in, and heard what you said you'd found out. I guess I was worried crazy, figured maybe McBride could scare Foxx off like Ted Marshall. So I went to see McBride. He wanted me with him to help, so I could tell Vega what he'd done. I thought it was going to be a beating, I swear that. McBride never told me. I guess it doesn't matter, I'm still an accessory. You know, he had this messenger uniform on, had that package. I didn't even ask about it! I figured he'd just gotten a messenger's job, actors do that. Maybe I was too worried about Rey to think. Anyway, Foxx wasn't home. McBride waited upstairs, sent me out to watch for Foxx. I was to signal when I saw Foxx coming. Only I saw Fortune, and beat it. I just ran. I forgot that was the signal— look up, and cross the street, when I saw Foxx. McBride only really wanted me there so I could be a witness, tell Rey what McBride had done for him."

I suppose everyone in that room was thinking the same —how crazy can a man be, Sean McBride; how stupid can a man be, Lehman. But it wasn't so stupid. Not if you put yourself in Lehman's place. Who would even dream that a man would kill just to get back into favor? Who would do it, except a half-sane, dull-minded, semi-savage given to impulses and violence he had never controlled, who hungered for a dream of success he had almost had in his fingers? McBride would have, yes, without a second thought, a hesitation.

Gazzo said, "That's why he thought Fortune was Foxx, you'd given the signal by mistake. Jesus!"

Emory Foxx was on his feet, out of the chair. "You don't believe that Lehman, do you? He's lying! All of it!"

24

EMORY FOXX laughed at us. "That's quite a story. Lehman should write TV scripts. Beautiful! You notice how it makes Vega pure as snow, and Mr. Lehman a poor, duped lamb? Everything done by Sean McBride—who happens to be conveniently dead and very silent. A really perfect story —for Ricardo Vega!"

Gazzo said, "An ex-con? He lies, risks going back to prison, loses everything he's made for a lot of years?"

"Lehman would do anything for Vega," Foxx snorted. "He's grateful. I've watched him bowing and scraping for years. Vega would pay him a fortune to save his yellow skin, and what does Lehman risk? That you don't believe the part about him not knowing McBride had a bomb. It's a risk, yes, but Vega would pay big, and if you believe Leman, he gets a slapped wrist."

I said, "I believe him, Foxx. In thirteen years neither Vega or Lehman tried to kill you. McBride is with Vega a few weeks, and he takes a bomb to you. It fits McBride alone."

"Vega never found an animal to do his killing before!"

Gazzo said, "That note McBride wrote, you have it, Lehman?"

Lehman took the note from his inner pocket. Gazzo read it. "It's handwritten, Foxx. It says what Lehman told us: McBride wanted to do Vega a favor by handling you, he wanted Lehman's help. We'll prove it's McBride's writing. Lehman's secretary is a witness. McBride alone bought the bomb materials; we checked. He made it in his room, all night like a crazy man, alone. No, McBride had the idea by himself."

"Ted Marshall, then!" Foxx said. "McBride hadn't been fired then. He was working for Vega. Maybe Vega found out that Marshall was helping to frame him. I saw McBride there—twice that night. I'm not lying, the superintendent saw him."

"He already told me he saw McBride," I admitted.

George Lehman said, "I don't know. Rey was pretty mad at Marshall, yeh. Before he found out about you, Foxx, he had the idea Marshall was working against him. He sent McBride to watch Marshall, and Fortune, and Fortune's girl—off and on. Rey blows a lot of steam, that's how he is. Maybe he said something about wanting Marshall off his back, and McBride did the same thing he tried with Foxx."

"It's a pattern," Gazzo said. "Men usually work, and kill, in a pattern."

"McBride went crazy when he beat a man," Lehman recalled. "When that friend of Marshall's was patching Marshall up after we beat him, he said McBride had almost killed him then. Maybe McBride thought Rey wanted Marshall 'handled' again, went and beat him around some more, and killed him. That could be where he got the idea to use the bomb next—nothing to lose."

I said, "My woman can tell things about McBride's violence, and impulse action. You're blinded by hate, Foxx. You want to hurt Vega any way you can, I know about that, believe me. Too much hate in you, Foxx."

"Too much?" Foxx said. "Too much hate? There isn't any hate too much for Vega, Fortune."

"What was it, Foxx?" Gazzo said. "Your reason? The D.A. never has told me the motive would shake a jury so hard."

Foxx seemed to shrink where he stood, said nothing.

"Lehman told me," I said. I told them everything Lehman had told me about Hollywood, the Congressional investigation, the blacklisting. "It's a sad story, but not enough for all Foxx has done for thirteen years. An obsession, magnified."

Emory Foxx sat down as if the memory of those years I had told about was too much weight. He looked at George Lehman. Lehman met his stare. Foxx licked at his lips, the heavy face twisted, the words he wanted to say somehow unable to come out. He looked at me, his voice hoarse when it came.

"Broke with Communism? Vega told them he'd broken with the Party, and he proved it?" Foxx said, looked around at all of us. "Did Lehman tell you *how* Vega proved he'd broken with Communism? Did he tell you that? No, he didn't tell you, he wouldn't."

All at once my neck began to crawl. A faint sensation, somehow aware of what was to come. "How, Foxx?"

Foxx watched Lehman. "He says Vega had no reason to want me out of his way. He's right. Vega was the new genius then. I wasn't in his way. He had it all going, a brilliant future. He has his brilliant future now, but at that moment back then he was afraid he'd lose it at the start. Down inside he's always been a coward, fearful he won't be on top someday."

"What did he do, Foxx?" Gazzo said.

Foxx laughed the coldest laugh I'd ever heard. "He proved he wasn't a Communist anymore, he was clean." His voice almost light, amused in a macabre way. "He proved it to those Congressmen by giving them every name of everyone who'd been Communists with him! He crawled on his belly to make them forgive him, let him go. He confessed everything about himself—and everything he knew about everyone else! His friends! He talked, and talked, and I was one of the names he talked about. They called me back. I wouldn't talk. So I went to jail, I was blacklisted for thirteen years, and Ricardo Vega went on to the top."

Lehman said, "He was scared, a kid from the slums of Havana. One slip, Foxx. He's a genius. One mistake."

"One mistake? Forgive him?" Foxx said. "He destroyed twenty men one way or the other, to save himself. He wasn't even really in danger, a small risk, but he wouldn't even take that risk. He volunteered to talk, babbled. To *please* that committee! And since then? He's been safe, but he kept me on the blacklist, used lawyers to keep me quiet, threatened everyone who might listen to me, or hire me!

He's got the power. I was a convicted Communist, so he's kept me silent for thirteen years. One mistake?"

Lehman had no more to say. It was a long time ago, and those had been frightened days for a lot of people, but how many had volunteered to destroy others to save themselves? Vega a little more scared—a kid from the Havana slums, to be understood? Would I have understood? Forgiven? I don't know. Maybe Foxx could be understood, forgiven.

"I'll go to jail?" Foxx said. "For framing Vega?"

"You'll go to jail," Gazzo said.

"Good," Foxx smiled, and it was a toad smile now. "A trial, right? A jury, newspapers, TV, magazines. I can tell my story at the trial. They'll print it now. No danger to print it when I tell it all in court. Vega is news. They'll do it big; magazine stories, the works. My story, Anne Terry's story, all about McBride. It all comes out. I'll get him after all!"

Thirteen years is a long time to hate, and to be frustrated. An obsession big enough to make him grasp at a frail straw to commit legal murder on Vega had to be fed.

"I guess you will," Gazzo said, "if anyone cares by now. You paid a hell of a price. Prison, and a dead wife."

Emory Foxx was pale for a moment. "We all die, Captain. She hadn't had much life since I went to prison anyway."

Gazzo waved an arm. "Take him and book him. Lehman, too."

Detectives took Foxx and Lehman out. The rest of the detectives left. Boone Terrell waited. After his own story had been told, Terrell had listened in silence. His impassive farmer's face had reacted only once—when Foxx told what Vega had done to him so long ago. Then Terrell had set his gaunt face in hard judgment on a man who betrayed his friends.

Gazzo said in the vacuum that seemed to hang over the dim room now, "The D.A. doesn't take to frame-ups, he won't go gentle on Foxx. The trial should be a circus all right. Vega'll find enemies he never even heard of."

"Lehman?" I said.

"He came in on his own. If the D.A. believes him, we might settle for a low guilty plea, suspend it."

"If he goes to trial, I can help. A jury should believe my story about him."

"Yeh, a patsy for Sean McBride and Vega," Gazzo said, and he looked at Boone Terrell. "You helped Foxx. You signed a false statement. Maybe your wife's death had you all mixed up. Go on home now, but stay close. I'll talk with the D.A. If he won't drop charges, we should get probation at least."

Terrell unwound his gaunt frame from the chair.

"I thank you, Captain," he said, and walked erect from the room.

I had a momentary vision of seeing him through the cafeteria window on the rainy night when it had all started for me. A vision of Anne Terry's face, gentle as she had looked at Terrell.

"She meant a lot to him," I said. "And she tried to give him something.'

Gazzo watched the door, and scowled into the room.

"I wish I'd met her. I've wished that since about halfway," Gazzo said. "A blackmailer, and a crazy fool!"

"You have a drink," I said, "and you wonder."

Gazzo's been a policeman for a long time. "They go through here like a parade, Dan. Sometimes the guilty, sometimes the victims, and the difference is a push one way or the other. She was born poor in a rich world; lived poor in a country that still believes in its Puritan lousy soul that the poor deserve to be poor! We gave her a crazy dream and no way to get it. I see that, too—every damned day. Most just dream, but some got to try. What did we give her to try with? A Senator who uses his power to squeeze a better deal than his neighbors; big companies that spend millions to con the public, and thousands to silence critics; blackmail in high places—except we call it influence, the payoff. She's tough, and strong, and never got past seventh grade, and she uses the weapon she finds! What the hell else do we expect with what we've given her?"

"Expect, Captain?" I said. "We expect her to be a good little girl, accept that she was supposed to be poor."

"Let the Ricardo Vegas use her, power her. Yeh."

"Not Anne Terry," I said. "Never passive, no. She had to act, shape her own life, even if it meant the end of her."

"You clear the smoke away, it's a common abortion, Foxx muddying it up, and a nut named Sean McBride," Gazzo said. "You know what gives me bad dreams, Dan? We get them all, the weak ones caught by circumstances, and the really dangerous one gets away."

"The abortionist," I said. "He was a professional, Gazzo; you'll get him someday."

"Yeh, after he maybe kills how many poor kids got nowhere else to turn the way our very moral citizens make it?"

"The rich can go to Japan, Denmark," I said.

"Swell," Gazzo said.

There was nothing more to say. Gazzo gave me my old gun with its bullets and I left. Boone Terrell was still in the corridor. He sat on the bench with Sarah Wiggen, and the two sleeping little girls. Sarah's face was flushed and smiling. She thanked me, and Terrell nodded his thanks.

"Gazzo'll go to bat for you," I said.

"I appreciate it," Terrell said.

"What do you do now?" I said.

Sarah said, "I'm going to move out with Boone. We're going to try, raise the children. I need something more than the job I settled for. Boone's going to try to work."

I didn't ask the obvious question, I didn't have to. Sarah had a bright glow to her face. She had come to like Boone Terrell over the last week. It was harder to tell with him. His face showed little. He had Anne Terry to forget; a very special woman, and he had loved her maybe too much.

"Sarah's a fine woman," Terrell said.

I saw Sarah wince. Just a little. It wasn't a "fine woman" she wanted to be to Terrell. She wanted to be what Anne had been, she probably always would. But she couldn't be, and a "fine woman" was at least a start.

"Can you find work up here, Boone?" I said.

"I reckon I can try," he said. "Last couple days I been thinkin'. Annie, she was a woman shook a man—like a head o' real powerful liquor. Like I was drunk on her. Annie was a strong female, and I never wanted to chance losin' her. If I don't need her, if the kids don't need her, maybe she leaves me, see? Maybe I knew that, you know, and didn't want to find work. Could be all this time I plain wanted to depend on Annie so she'd stay around. Could be my leg ain't so bad, I could find work don't pain it much."

We all seemed to think about that for a time. Sarah stood and began to wrap the little girls in their blankets to carry them out. I said my good-bys, told Boone I was sure he'd find work, told both of them they'd be okay.

Maybe they would be. Sarah could be a different woman if she had a purpose, and Terrell was a simple man. Sally Anne and Aggy could even get a better life out of it. Sarah might get some things of Anne's after all. Good can come from bad, sometimes.

25

I CALLED Marty from a tavern. There was no answer. I took the subway home. She was waiting in my bedroom when I came in. She had the heat on to welcome me.

"I called Gazzo's office," she said, smiled. "They told me you were there, so I came to wait. Is it over, Dan?"

"Over," I said.

I dropped my clothes on a chair. My broken ribs hurt, my leg ached, and I looked like a bandaged mummy, but I got into bed. I was shaken, drained. It was all over. Vega could walk tall, and Anne Terry was gone for good. She was no longer with me. She had ended like a fading note of music that slips into silence leaving ony the memory of an echo.

I told Marty about it all. I needed to talk, and I needed Marty. Two people are always worlds apart no matter how close. Minute to minute you have to find each other again, before separate needs and weaknesses tear you apart. Everyone must have somewhere to rest. So I told her, talked it out of me.

"Boone Terrell and Sarah Wiggen might even make it," I said. "Good for those kids, anyway. Anne Terry did what she had to do, and she was a good mother, but the kids are different people. They have to find their own way, and it might be easier for them in the end this way."

She gave me a cigarette. "Vega comes out all free?"

"Like a virgin," I said. "There we all were in that room clearing Ricardo Vega. All the little flies food for the toad. In our own trouble, or dead, yet saving the golden idol. We had to do it—for truth, justice, morality. But the result was all for Vega. It's a lousy world."

"Not lousy, Dan, just not very fair. But who said that the world was supposed to be fair? Who said it could be fair?"

"No one, I suppose," I said, and I held her. "Maybe it's not such a bad world. I've got you. You and me, even if the abortionist goes free."

"A simple abortion after all? Vega not involved?"

"Only Ted Marshall and some abortionist he knew. Marshall arranged it all, Anne told Boone Terrell that. Marshall fixed it, paid for it, and Anne—"

I stopped talking. Marty kissed me in the warm bed. I put out my cigarette. I sat up. Words marched around in my mind. Voices, words, phrases filling my head.

"Dan?" Marty said. "What is it?"

"I'm not sure. All of a sudden I'm hearing voices, small pieces of conversation," I said. "Where did Ted Marshall get the money to pay a professional abortionist? That costs money, a lot of money. Marshall barely had beer money."

"You're sure, Dan?"

"He lived on his mother," I said. I got out of the warm bed, began to dress. "I'm sorry, baby; you go on home. This could take a while."

"I'll stay here," she said.

I put on my old duffle coat, and the black beret this time to keep my bandaged head warm in the early morning hours. I reloaded my cannon, slipped it into a coat pocket, and kissed Marty before I left.

There was light under the apartment door. It was late for light. I rang the bell, put my hand back into my pocket. This time, no mistakes.

When he opened the door, he was fully dressed. The votive lights flickered behind him. It didn't look like he'd been asleep much for some days. The skin of his dark, girlish face seemed drawn, like parchment over a skull. He tried for lightness.

"So late, Mr. Fortune? It got to be me you want this time, yes? I never know you swing like that."

"I don't, but it doesn't make me proud," I said. "Can I come in, Madero? The police have the case all solved. I thought you'd like to hear about it."

"They have who kill Ted?"

"They have it worked out," I said.

161

He backed inside, bowed me in after him. The ascetic, medieval room hadn't changed. Fresh votive lights burned under all the crucifixes. Madero sat down on the biggest throne-chair, his slender body lost in its massive back and arms. I took a smaller high-backed throne.

"Who kill Ted?" Madero asked. "Why?"

"Sean McBride," I said. "We're not so sure why. There's a few things I can't make fit. You knew Marshall better than anyone. Maybe you can help me."

"Ted was my friend," he said. "I try."

I told him the whole story as it had worked out. He listened with his serious, public manner. He showed little reaction to any of it until I got to McBride. Then he leaned forward, and there was something like an angry hiss deep in his throat.

"That Sean McBride! I hated him when he beat Ted."

"An animal," I said. "We should have known, I guess. You told me you saw him that night here."

"Yes, I see him."

"You talked to him in the lobby, threatened him."

"Yes, I see him hang around. I throw him out."

"He came back, it looks like," I said. "Ted Marshall had Anne's abortion done for her, right? You knew, didn't you? He was cracking all the way."

Madero nodded sadly. "I know he do it. He try to help Anne. He don't mean to kill."

"No," I said. "He paid for it, even. I wonder where he got the money?"

Madero shrugged. "I don't know."

"He didn't have much money," I said. "The Medical Examiner said the abortion was a good job, professional. Real skill, and that costs money. A trained man did the work, her death was a small mistake, the wrong pills. A real doctor, maybe."

"Just like a real doctor," Madero said. "Maybe some guy never got no real chance to be doctor."

I nodded. "Just what I was thinking. A medical student, maybe. Maybe an army medical corpsman who worked a lot with doctors. The job was that good. Someone who should have been a doctor, maybe."

"Some guys never get no chance," he said, a little bitter.

"No breaks. A man with skill no one will let him use, held down when he should have been using his talent."

"Nobody helps," he said. "Everybody laughs—look who wants to be doctor. I know."

"That's right," I said, "you weren't always a super, were you, Frank? What were you? A medical student? An army corpsman helping out in operations? An operating room nurse?"

The tight skin seemed to stretch thinner over his girlish face, his dark eyes sank almost out of sight in the flickering light of the votive candles. He said nothing. Eyes on me.

"In Cuba, maybe? Or here," I said. "George Lehman said you patched up Marshall after Lehman and McBride beat him. Marshall was pretty badly banged around; most people would have been afraid to touch him. You patched him up. What do you have, a bag of instruments stolen from a hospital?"

"You got to be crazy," Madero said.

"No, Frank, I don't think so. Anne Terry told her husband that the abortionist was someone Ted Marshall knew. Emory Foxx spoke of 'them' when he reported Ted talking about what had happened, about where the operation was done. Ted spoke in the plural; two men in it all together. Ted had no money, and Anne Terry had some two hundred dollars—which she didn't spend; she made no big withdrawals recently. Yet the job was pretty good. That should have cost money, real money. It didn't because it was done *free*, by a friend—you."

"You go out of here now!" Madero said.

I produced my big pistol. He looked at it, licked his lips. I wasn't being surprised this time.

"That first day I met you, you came in like a man with a problem. You were both nervous, something going on between you and

Marshall; I saw it. You covered, and I thought it was sexual, but Marshall wasn't your lover. What was between you was the abortion, the danger you were both in. You're a super, that room is close. You're in the best position to have known, and used, that empty room. You admitted knowing Anne Terry."

"It is all lies!"

"The police will find your medical background, and they'll find your instruments, unless you got rid of them, which I doubt. Those instruments are your dream—the medical man. The super on Hudson Street will talk now. There were fingerprints all over that room; some will be yours."

His long lashes flicked at each point I made as if they were blows. He had stopped looking at my pistol.

He said, "In Cuba I want to be medical student. A doctor where I live, the slum, he like me. He say I am a bright boy, he teach me many things. With Batista I have no chance to be student. The doctor, my friend, helps me to be medical soldier. I learn very much. When revolution came I am Batista soldier, so I must run. I come here, work in hospital. Only orderly, but I watch, listen, read books. There is Cuban doctor who lets me watch operations. I take instruments. I get laid off. I start to help people have little money, need medical help."

"Abortions, Frank? Before Anne?"

"All kinds of medicine help," he said. "Some girls want help, so I do. I think if I can make enough money maybe I can go to medical school even now, but—"

"Tell me about Anne?"

The pain in his dark eyes was almost physical. "Ted ask I help. No money. I do to help Ted, and the girl! A friend! I have seen doctors use those pills. I don't know that they are bad with so much pentothal! She is sick, I don't know."

"I believe you," I said. "An accident. Was killing Ted Marshall an accident, too?"

164

26

HE WAS UP. "No!"

I waved my big cannon. "Sit down, Frank."

He sat, his eyes sunk into his parchment face. "You say McBride kill Ted! Yes! You say police know!"

"I said they had it worked out as McBride," I said. "I didn't say they were right. You killed Marshall, Frank."

He shook his head, back and forth, no and no and no! His eyes looked at his votive lights, a slender moth devoted to the flickering light that was going to somehow help him.

"You've already told me," I said. "You admit seeing Sean McBride that night. You admit being in the lobby, telling him to get out. But that night, Frank, before I found Marshall's body, you'd told me only that you'd seen McBride maybe three hours earlier! You didn't mention that you'd seen McBride in the lobby at eight-thirty. You implied that you'd just come home around nine-forty. You hadn't; you'd been in the building all along."

"So I was there. It don't mean nothing."

"You wanted to hide it," I said. "And if you were there, then you had to have heard me yelling in the cellar! You heard me, and you didn't come to free me. You didn't come to me, because you wanted me out of the way, too. Emory Foxx saw you there that night, and you saw him. You probably saw Foxx and Marshall carry me down. You listened to Foxx and Marshall talk in Marshall's apartment. You heard Marshall spill his guts to Foxx, tell him everything, even where the abortion was done."

I stopped to let it sink in, but Madero didn't speak. He just sat there now with his sunken eyes lost, his dark face so taut I thought it would split open.

I said, "Ted Marshall was stupid enough to try to help Foxx frame Ricardo Vega, but you're not that stupid. You knew Marshall had become dangerous. He'd told Foxx enough to hang himself, and he was ready to tell the whole world. He was about to break, you couldn't trust him any longer. No one could have in his state. So you went in after Foxx left, and you killed him then."

In day-to-day life you can't see people change, not usually. Change is too slow, too imperceptible. But now, as I watched, Frank Madero changed before my eyes like those flowers you see opening in stop-time photography. He had been taut, sunken, lost, shrinking into oblivion in that enormous medieval chair. By some trick of my mind, and the flickering votive lights, he seemed to grow again, swell, blossom like a chrysalis emerging from a dried shell. His face relaxed, his eyes came out of their shadow, a look of sudden peace over him.

"I go in," he said. "Ted he shake. I tell him I hear what he say to Foxx. He fall to pieces, sit down, hide his face, say he can't take no more. I have hammer with me. I hit him. I drag him to window. It is hard, but I get him up on window. I am more strong than you know. I push him out. I close window, come back down to here."

"Your friend," I said, "but he would have ruined you."

I stood, the pistol ready. "We better go, Frank."

He smiled that soft, girlish smile. His hand went into a pocket. Some sixth sense told me—that sudden relaxation, that peace on his face. The change a moment before because he had made his decision. His hand came out of his pocket.

I dove, swung the pistol at his arm.

He screamed as the pistol hit, the small capsule flying out of his hand to the floor. He didn't try to attack me. He slid to the floor, scrambled toward the capsule. I stumbled against the chair, swore, recovered. His groping hand reached the capsule on the floor. I hit him with the pistol. He fell flat on his face, groaned where he lay on the floor. I got the capsule, dropped it into the kitchen sink, ran the water, and leaned on the sink breathing hard.

He lay prone on the floor, his arms spread out, unmoving. He began to cry.

Captain Gazzo was still in his office, finishing the paper work this night had handed him. He listened to me, and to Frank Madero. His nostrils flared—he liked a complete case; he so rarely got one. He had his abortionist.

As Frank Madero finished his story, Ricardo Vega strode into the office. Vega was rumpled and unshaven, just released and angry. He had some words for Gazzo.

"I'm talking to my lawyers, Gazzo. An official statement to the newspapers about your stupidity might make me—"

"We had a case. You were framed," Gazzo said. "We worked and cleared you. We might make something of coercion of McBride; don't push it. Foxx goes to jail, that's all. Go on, Madero."

Vega's face darkened. He didn't go on, but he didn't leave. He stood waiting.

Frank Madero said, "That's all. I kill my friend. I just want to be a doctor. No chance. I don't mean the girl to die. I do a good job, have one mistake. I would be good doctor. When I come here, you know how I come? I hide in wheels of airplane. I almost freeze. My brother, too, but he don't make it. He fall out of wheels of plane over ocean. No one know except me. My mother in Cuba have twelve kids. What is one?"

Vega looked at Madero at the mention of Cuba. Curiosity, an idea to use in a play. Madero saw Vega watching him.

"I know him," Madero said. "You know something? We come from same slum in Havana. We both want to be much, to do much. He get help at start, I get nothing. That is the difference."

"You are nothing, *amigo*," Vega said; "that's the difference. I got out of that slum because I was more than the others, and because I had guts. Don't cry to me."

Gazzo said, "Get the hell out of here, Vega."

Ricardo Vega hesitated, ready to battle. Then he flashed that bantering grin, bowed to Gazzo, and walked out.

I signed my formal statement, and so did Frank Madero. They took Madero out. Gazzo leaned back in his chair.

"Thanks, Dan. I'll sleep better."

"You'd have found him. Sean McBride didn't quite fit when you thought about it. Not for Ted Marshall. Too soon. He only went crazy after Vega fired him, his chance gone."

"Maybe," Gazzo agreed. "And maybe not. McBride fitted good enough for Marshall's killing. We've got too many cases to dig into the reasonably solved ones."

I had no good answer to that. Gazzo knows the limitations of his work better than I do. So I left once more.

Outside on the misty streets only a few late citizens hurried along to their unknown destinations. A big Cadillac stood at the curb. Ricardo Vega rolled down a back window, called to me. The driver was someone new.

"You're a good detective, Fortune. They told me about it," Vega said. "No more trouble between us, all right? We were both wrong. I'd like to pay you something."

"What do you want me to do for you?" I asked.

He smiled his winning smile: the *hidalgo*. "Just don't make me sound so bad at Foxx's trial. Tell only what you have to. After all, what did I do we all don't do?"

"But you'll tell everything yourself," I said. "If Lehman goes to trial, it'll go better for him if you tell the jury everything that made him do what he did. How you used him, and for what."

"Lehman acted on his own, just like that crazy McBride. He gets no help from me, Fortune. Why should he?"

"Funny. That's what he said you'd do."

"Did he?" Vega said, less friendly.

I said, "Don't pay me anything, Vega. I'm going to get it all into the record at Foxx's trial. All I can about Anne Terry, Lehman, McBride,

Foxx, myself and even Marty. Marty's how I started on the case, so I'll get her in. I'm going to crucify you as far as I can."

His dark eyes glittered. "I can still hurt Marty."

"No, we know too much now. We know your weaknesses. You'll stay far away from us."

I turned to walk away. I was tired of him. He spoke behind me.

"You know, I really liked her, Fortune. Anne Terry, I mean. She had beauty, talent, strength. I got closer to her than to any girl in a long time. I already told you that. We were good together. Maybe I should even have married her."

I turned back. "You're telling me something?"

"I'm telling you that I didn't try to do all of it, that I didn't want to do it. She was just too much. I am what I am. I won't be pushed, and I can't share what I am. I can't share Ricardo Vega. With no one."

I heard what Anne Terry had said on that rainy night, and what Emory Foxx had said tonight—Vega would never be sure. The difference between a born prince and a success-prince. A born prince knew he would always be a prince. Rey Vega would never be sure what tomorrow would make him. So he worked for himself alone, his talent directed inward, his work unrelated to anything but his own victory. He could only use people, and nothing connected him inside to Frank Madero from the same Havana slum. But work must go outward, not inward, and Rey Vega would stand isolated, afraid of the next "Vega" behind him.

"They say you're a genius," I said to him. "I always believed them. Maybe you could be a genius: you've got skill and talent. But you're not a genius. You need too many flies to feed you. You haven't had a moment of daring since you put your own money into your work. You're dancing for the public now, and you're going to fade before more original artists. You don't have the vision or the courage to be great. You can't want women; you can only chase skirts. A life of one-night stands. Side-show genius."

His handsome face had been framed in the open car window as I talked. Now his head turned as if to give orders to the new man behind the wheel of his car. I braced, thought: here we go again? But he didn't speak. Not to the driver, and not to me. He gave a faint shrug, a half-smile, and vanished back inside his Cadillac. The big car slipped silently away. I watched until it turned a corner, and then I began to walk.

When I reached an avenue, I looked through the mist for a taxi. I wanted Marty now: my place, my haven. One more fly with desperate hopes and no hope. Other times, other places, Francisco Madero might have been a hero, needed. He might have saved lives and been honored, instead of losing a life and being forever damned. A moment of error, and then the fear that had killed Ted Marshall. I wasn't going to be the one who had to look at Mrs. Marshall's eyes when she heard the reason for her son's death.

I was going home to Marty where it would be warm and we could smile close in the dark. I had a woman, not just a skirt to hang in my closet overnight. Ricardo Vega could have had a woman, but he was afraid to lose himself. A rich man who was, of course, a better man, so could live only for himself, afraid to touch.

A solitary taxi came far down the deserted avenue. I watched its top light distant in the mist. Ricardo Vega could have had a real woman. If he had been a little more man, and a little less prince of success, Anne Terry could have had her chance and none of it would have happened. I felt sad, even bitter, but she would never stand still for that. Not Anne Terry. She would cheer me up: "Forget it, Gunner; we all die. You got to take risks. At least the kids'll be okay." A girl no better and no worse than most.

No! That was a lie, an insult. I heard her scorn: "Get away from me with that cheap crap, Gunner!"

No. She had been much worse than most, and a lot better than most. She hadn't made the conditions of her life, so she had refused to accept the conditions. For her own needs she should have left her kids in Arkansas, but she hadn't. For the small pleasures she should have made the best of what she had, but she wouldn't. Her life had given her little to battle with, so she faced the weapons she had to use, and used them. A woman who shaped her own life if it killed her.

The taxi reached me still empty. I sat back, and I didn't feel good. She was slipping away forever, Anne Terry. In a few days, weeks, I would forget her like a puddle that dried and vanished after a rainy night. A vague memory, and I realized as I looked at the dark night city outside the taxi that I had been working all along for a miracle. Not to solve a case, or catch a killer. Not for justice or truth. I had been working to make her live again, to bring her back, to let her win this time. I had been working to give her another chance. This isn't a world of miracles, yet I felt that I had failed her, too.

After a time the cab passed a big Cadillac in the mist. It could have been Ricardo Vega's Cadillac. I stared at it. I felt a sudden surge of wolfish joy. I was going to "get" Vega at the trial. I felt better. At least revenge. I'm human, too.

THE END

**Read the first chapter
of the next exciting Dan Fortune mystery**

Walk a Black Wind
by Dennis Lynds
#4 in the Edgar Award-winning Dan Fortune mystery series

"One of the Year's Best Mysteries"
– The New York Times
– The National Observer

Most of us pass through life without ever meeting real danger or fear. We slide from day to day, and nothing very bad happens. We like it that way, I think, even if we do sometimes feel that life is flat. But fear and horror come to some of us, and we meet it in different ways.

The man who arrived in my one-window office that Thursday in late October had seen fear or horror or both.

"Two weeks ago I met a girl," he said. "She's dead, Mr. Fortune, murdered. I want her murderer caught."

He was my height, about five-foot-ten, broad and solid in a good blue pin-striped business suit under a navy topcoat. His olive-colored face was faintly Latin, clean-shaven and deeply lined, but somehow youthful despite the deep wrinkles. I guessed his age at about forty-five. He held a blue homburg in both hands as he settled into my one extra chair. His thick hair was dark brown and coarse. There was no gray in the hair, and his hat was unusual these days. The business card he placed on my old desk explained the hat: John F. Andera, Sales Representative, Marvel Office Equipment, Inc. Salesmen were among the few who still always wore hats.

"What was the girl to you, Mr. Andera?" I said.

His eyes were a cloudy blue as if he had been stunned. He looked like a man who has been hit by a train and isn't sure yet what damage has been done. Not sure if he was alive or dead, holding himself together inside, breathing carefully.

"A friend," he said. "I liked her. I had ... hopes."

He spoke with a kind of stiff, prep-school diction that was not natural to him. The sound of some faint accent underneath.

I said, "What was the name originally? My grandfather was Fortunowski when he got off the ship. Sometimes I miss it."

He didn't smile. "Anderoparte. We came from Corsica. My father changed it for business. Will you take the job?"

"I'll have to hear more about it," I said. "You only knew this girl for two weeks?"

He glanced around my cubicle office with its view of an air shaft wall as if he was surprised I'd think twice about any job. With the shabby office, my rough clothes, and my missing arm, I don't look affluent, and we are a world based on cash and prospects. Andera had expected me to be hungry to work, but he said nothing. He took two newspaper clippings from his pocket and gave them to me.

They were both from *The New York Times.* The first was from yesterday's late edition, Wednesday. An inch on page nine:

Woman Found Murdered

NEW YORK. Fran Martin, 280 East Eighty-fourth Street, was found stabbed to death in her bed at 8:30 A.M. this morning by her cleaning woman. Police report that the victim died sometime after midnight last night. No motive is yet known for the brutal slaying of the woman who worked as a cocktail waitress at the Emerald Room on East Sixty-sixth Street. Police are investigating.

The second clipping was much longer, dated Thursday, today, and had run on page two of the *Times:*

Murder Victim Daughter
of Upstate Mayor

NEW YORK. The attractive young victim of Tuesday night's slaying at 280 East Eighty-fourth Street has now been identified as Francesca Crawford, daughter of Mayor Martin J. Crawford of Dresden, New York.

Mayor Crawford revealed that his daughter had left home three months ago, and had not been in contact with their family since. He could offer no explanation for her living in Manhattan under an assumed name. The mayor and his wife are now in seclusion at The Plaza hotel.

Miss Crawford, first identified as "Fran Martin," was found stabbed in her bed …

The rest was a repeat of the first story, with more words but no more facts. I handed the clippings back to John Andera.

"Any ideas why she was killed?" I asked him.

"No, none," he said. "I met Fran two weeks ago today at a party. She was alone, I took her to a late dinner. I liked her. I took her out twice more. We … got along. She seemed much older, more mature, than she really was."

"How old was she?"

"Twenty, Mr. Fortune. Just twenty. I went away a few days on business this week and returned on Wednesday for a date with Fran. She didn't show at the restaurant. I was angry, so I didn't call her. Today I saw that second story." His thick hands shook. "She had been using a false name. Then she was dead. I had hoped … well, that we …" He stopped.

"You can prove you were out of town?"

"Yes, of course." He had expected the question, and he anticipated my next one. "I'm not married, I have no jealous women, and I don't know if she had other men. I don't know anything, that's why I want you. I can pay well."

"For a girl you hardly knew?"

"How long does a man have to know a girl to know he likes her? I liked her a lot! I'll pay you a thousand dollars in advance, another thousand when you bring in her murderer!"

His voice was still steady, but inside he was bleeding hard where it didn't show but hurt just as much. Inside, he was crying for a girl who hadn't even given him her right name. Then, that wasn't so unusual in the fast world of New York.

"That's a lot of money," I said. "You could get a big agency for that, and the police will handle it well enough."

"The police have too much work, and I don't want Fran lost in a big agency's computers. I want a man who will work for Francesca. I want to do something!"

"It's still a lot of money," I said.

"Yes, it is. Because I want to make you take the job, and because I want my name kept out of it. I don't want to be involved," he said it bluntly. Either he was naive or bolder than he looked.

"Even though you can prove you were out of town?'

"I'm not worried about being thought guilty," he said. "It's just that a young girl, a salesman, a few weeks, you understand?"

I understood. The newspapers, and his office people, would have a fun time with it. We love to see dirt.

"All right," I said. "In murder, I have to work with the police. If I can't keep you out, I'll tell you first."

Andera thought for a moment, then nodded, and stood up. He counted ten hundred-dollar bills from his wallet. They were all new bills, he'd been prepared.

"I'll come here for any reports," he said.

When he was gone, I thought about him. He had paid me more than I was worth on any market, and I had a hunch that he knew it. Had he decided how much it would cost to make me take a case I didn't quite believe? Maybe, but did that mean that his story wasn't true, or only that he was afraid I wouldn't think it was true?

The only way to know was to go to work, and I could always use two thousand dollars. I called Center Street. They told me Captain Gazzo was on the case. It figured – a mayor's daughter cruelly murdered. A lieutenant wasn't important enough.

Gazzo agreed to meet me at the Medical Examiner's Building on the East River.

Meet the Author:
Dennis Lynds

A raconteur and Renaissance man, Dennis Lynds changed the mystery form and along the way created colorful private detectives who consistently won awards as well as the hearts of readers. He was a tall, lanky man with a nose the size of Gibraltar and a generous nature that made him a soft touch for friends, panhandlers, and his children. He published some 40 novels under various pseudonyms, won awards such as the Edgar, the mystery world's highest honor, and received accolades from legendary authors like Ross Macdonald. "A novelist of power and quality, ... one of the major imaginative creators in the crime field," Macdonald wrote of him.

The New York Times named several of Lynds's novels to its Best Mysteries of the Year lists. Remarkably, two of them written under different pseudonyms appeared on the same list – *Silent Scream* by Michael Collins and *Circle of Fire* by Mark Sadler.

Amused, Lynds said that none of the *Times* editors realized he was both Collins and Sadler. "I don't think they ever figured it out," he explained. And he never bothered to tell them.

Seldom does an author change the course of a genre once; rarely twice. Lynds is credited with being the writer who, in the late 1960s and early 1970s, propelled the detective novel into the Modern Age. His most famous pen name was Michael Collins. With that name, he created the opinionated Dan Fortune, the star of one of America's longest-running private detective series. The first book, *Act of Fear*, won the Edgar Allan Poe Award for Best First Novel. "Many critics believe Dan Fortune to be the culmination of a maturing process that transformed the private eye from the naturalistic Spade (Dashiell

Hammett) through the romantic Marlowe (Raymond Chandler) and the psychological Archer (Ross Macdonald) to the sociological Fortune," according to *Private Eyes: 101 Knights* by Robert Baker and Michael Nietzel.

At heart, Lynds was a rebel. Two decades later, he rattled mystery critics and changed the field again, this time by introducing literary techniques into the genre, beginning in the late 1980s with *Red Rosa, Castrato*, and *Chasing Eights*, and continuing well into the 1990s with *The Irishman's Horse, Cassandra in Red*, and *The Cadillac Cowboy*. Other authors followed, proving the flexibility and durability of the suspense world. "No one could accuse [Lynds] of reworking the same turf in his novels... . His last several books have pushed the private-eye form into some fascinating new shapes," according to *The Wall Street Journal* in 2000. *The Los Angeles Times* commented, "It takes style to bring that off. Bravery, too, of course."

Lynds also published mainstream novels, short stories, and poetry. Five of his literary short stories were honored in *Best American Short Stories*.

During World War II, he was a rifleman and carried books of poetry in his knapsack as he fought across France. He was a strong swimmer, so when he and fellow infantrymen were surrounded by Nazis, he plunged into an icy river, leading them to escape. He earned two Purple Hearts and a Bronze Star. Later he graduated with a degree in chemistry from Hofstra and a masters degree in journalism from Syracuse. A lifelong New Yorker, in the mid 1960s he finally left the East Coast's bitter winters to settle in the warm sunshine of Southern California. He was married three times, to Doris Flood, then Sheila McErlean, and finally to Gayle Hallenbeck Stone Lynds. He had two daughters, Katie and Deirdre Lynds, and two step children, Paul and Julia Stone.

Dennis Lynds died at age 81 in 2005. Jack Adrian wrote in *The Financial Times*, "Unusually for a mystery writer – as a breed, they tend to favor things as they are, rather than as they might be – the American author Dennis Lynds, politically, came from left of center.

This did not mean he preached bloody revolution. He wrote to entertain." Entertainment was something Lynds never forgot, that and to be generous to his friends.

Obituaries celebrating his work appeared around the globe. In a typical understatement, he commented near the end of his life, "I had a good run." His career had lasted more than fifty years.

Night of the Toads
#3 in the Edgar Award–winning Dan Fortune mystery series

by Dennis Lynds
Originally published under the pseudonym Michael Collins

Nude Actress Vanishes

NEW YORK. Anne Terry, 22, actress and model, who made headlines when she appeared nude for a whole act in a banned production at the New Player's Theater, was reported missing late last night.

The disappearance of the curvy actress was reported by her sister, Sarah Wiggen, of 29 West Seventy-sixth Street, who told police her "sexpot" sister vanished last Thursday from her West Tenth Street apartment.

The one time Dan Fortune met Anne Terry, she made a memorable impression on him. She was not only gorgeous, but she radiated a bold spirit, the kind that signaled bravery and honesty, and he admired that. Reading about her disappearance in the morning newspaper, he remembers with disgust how Ricardo Vega, the Broadway impresario, had verbally humiliated her when she tried to reignite their affair. Vega is "Rey" Vega to anyone who claims to know him well – El Rey, the King. He's handsome, rich, and powerful, and he always gets his way.

Sitting there, holding the newspaper, Fortune feels a tide of hot jealousy sweep through him. Rey has set his sights on another beautiful actress – Martine Adair, the woman Fortune loves, and his lover. Until now, she's resisted, and Fortune wants to protect her from the power plays that Rey is known for. Fortune has something going for him, too. He's a private detective, seasoned, and angry. If Rey had something to do with Anne Terry's disappearance, Fortune will find out, and he'll use what he knows to stop the bastard from hurting Marty.

Unfaltering suspense and vivid characterizations make this tale of the 1970s theater world in New York riveting. Here is an understanding of human weaknesses, a feeling for life in a great city, and an illuminating examination of the values we all live by that give this novel its unusual power.

"Tough, believable." – *San Francisco Examiner*

"Really moving … emotional soundness without sentimentality." – *San Francisco Chronicle*

"[Lynds] handles an excellent and complex plot with ease." – *The Washington Star*

"In the American private-eye tradition of Chandler, Hammett, and Macdonald." – *The New York Times Book Review*

###

75596799R00108

Made in the USA
Middletown, DE
06 June 2018